# The Owl on the Road to Medford

## *A Novella in Seven Stories*

## By Ann Littlewood

# Acknowledgements

The title story in this collection, *The Owl on the Road to Medford*, was the first place winner in the 2014 Oregon Writer's Colony short story contest. It was subsequently published in CALYX, A Journal of Art and Literature by Women, Summer/Fall 2016 , Vol. 29:2. The story is slightly revised for this novella.

I would like to acknowledge the kind assistance of Lacy Campbell in reviewing the manuscript for current wildlife rehabilitation practices.

My writing group was, as always, invaluable–Evan Lewis, Douglas Levin, Marilyn McFarlane, Cindy Brown, and especially Angela Sanders, who led me through the labyrinth of self-publishing. Christine Finlayson had many thoughtful suggestions that improved these stories considerably.

My wingman, Lee Littlewood, designed the cover.

This collection is dedicated to all those who work so hard to make a better world for wildlife and to those who love and lose and carry on anyway.

# Contents

# The Owl on the Road to Medford

The juvenile green heron, all beak and long fragile bones, fought every bite of herring I poked down its gullet. It was late, the Closed sign was up, and the clinic doorbell buzzed anyway. They must have seen my car or the light in the back room. Damn. I set the heron back in its cage and said, "If you barf all that up, I'll rip your beak right off." A waste of breath. This one never listened.

No doubt another effing robin. We'd taken in a dozen already, also an armada of baby mallards, eight scrub jays squalling for Mom, and three still-blind squirrels squirming in a heap. Springtime—when humans get their hands on wildlife too young to escape and haul them to the local wildlife rehab center.

A couple at the door. The woman held—as ever—a cardboard box. Miller Genuine Draft 24 pack, duct tape all over it. "Evening," I said. "What you got there?"

She looked me up and down, beard to boots, and frowned as if I was not what she had in mind. She shifted the box and said, "We found this bird in the road. The gas station guy said you'd take care of it. It was just sitting there where somebody would run over it."

The man said, "Innerstate 5. Southbound, at the roadside rest area south of Eugene. Some kind of chicken hawk. It's too young to fly." To her—"Give it to him and let's go."

"I couldn't just leave it there," the woman said, and looked sideways at him with her eyes narrow.

His mouth twitched, sour. "We're here, aren't we?"

Late twenties, maybe, both of them, and raised poor. Everyone in Oregon wears tee shirts and running shoes and jeans in summer, but their front teeth gave them away. His were chipped, hers crowded. That, and their hair. His thick ponytail poked out under a faded Mariners cap, she had two inches of brown pushing yellow away. Broke for a good while.

And both of them tired and cranky. Way cranky.

No sense of danger, even though I was alone. Too road-weary and wrapped up in their own problems. Dollar bills in the donation jar weren't worth a scuffle. Anyway, I'm big enough that no one bothers me, not without giving it some thought.

Looked like they wouldn't be together long. She'd leave him as soon as they got where they were going. I could see it coming.

She said, hanging onto the box, "Are you the night person or what?"

"I'm the director. Everyone else has gone home. Let's take a look."

She followed the box as I took it and set it on the counter. He stayed at the door. "Stinks in here."

Of course it stinks. Bird shit and bait herring and feeder mice. The chlorine disinfectant is the worst. Get over it.

I tore off the tape and opened it up, careful of my eyes. You never know what's going to bust out talons-first. But this bird sagged in a corner, one wing drooping. Eight inches of speckled brown feathers with tufts on top of its head. "It's a screech owl."

The woman made a little snort and muttered, "Chicken hawk, my ass."

The guy crossed his arms over his chest—blurry dark tattoos. "What do *you* know? I've seen owls. They're bigger." Talking to her.

"Owls come in all sizes," I said, trying to paper over hostility with information. Waste of breath. I reached in and wrapped a hand around the bird's legs up close to its body, careful not to damage it further. It snapped its beak once, no fight in it. I laid it on its back on the counter, the woman leaning close and the man watching, too. The breast felt solid with muscle, not starved down. Good. A recent disaster. With my free hand, I worked gently along the thin bones hidden under feathers, testing for the tiny crunching wiggle that means a break. Crepitation, it's called. Creepy word. "Wings are okay." The legs were fine, too. I checked the eyes. One big yellow eye had blood in it. "Concussed. I'll get it to the vet tomorrow. Probably hit by a car." I straightened up. "Minding its own business and got clobbered out of nowhere."

The guy said, "That happens every day. Every damn day."

When I can, I tell people they did right by trying to help a wild creature. Sometimes it's a pitch for a donation. Not this time, but still. "It's stunned and can't hunt. It would have died out there. Here, it'll be safe and fed and have a chance. We'll set it free if we can. That's what we do here."

That always eases people, and it did for her. The guy relaxed, too, but kept the impatience. "We gotta go. We got a lot of miles ahead."

"Where to?" I asked, to be polite.

He said, "Medford, land of milk and honey. Or so I'm told."

She snapped, "Land where *one* of us can get a job."

I folded up the wings to carry the owl to the back room.

He said, "You got what you want, like always, so quit stalling and let's go."

"What I *want* is not have to fix *your* problems. You can't ask me to raise—"

"Shit." I didn't intend to say it aloud. I wanted them gone.

"What?" She turned away from him and crowded me to see the bird.

I touched its lower belly. "Didn't see it right off. This big pink spot with no feathers? Brood patch. She's been sitting on eggs. Or chicks."

She stepped back and frowned. Wide brown eyes looked a question at me.

I dodged it. "Good timing for her to show up. We've got a screech owl youngster in back. It can imprint on this one." She followed me behind the counter into the back room without asking. Not allowed, but I let it go. After a few seconds, I heard him step after us.

I set the newcomer next to the half-grown chick in a plastic box. The couple stared at the two owls, wild animals catching people's attention the way they do, while I fetched a few cut-up mouse pieces and laid them in front of the birds. Maybe one or the other would eat on its own.

The new owl leaned against the side, blotto.

The woman rocked on her heels, uneasy. "What about her babies?" She wasn't going to let it go.

"The dad might handle it. The males help out."

"He couldn't do it alone." The guy was dead certain. "No way."

The woman's hands clenched to fists. "We gotta take her back where we found her."

I shook my head. "She's too out of it to survive."

"But her babies will die."

The guy said, "You can't save every single one." Not sarcastic, just saying it.

"You absolutely got that right." She chewed on her lower lip, scowling.

He said, "It's not right I have to choose."

What?

She ignored him and watched the owls. "I could find the exact spot where we picked her up."

I started wondering if I'd have to fight her for the bird. "If the chicks hatched already, they'll get hungry and start food-calling. You know how it is to hear a baby crying? How you have to make the baby happy so it'll stop? The male will hear that and feed them. If the hunting's good, he'll manage." The bigger babies would likely eat the littler ones, but some information just isn't helpful.

She studied me, skeptical.

The orphan owl let out a cheep. "Like that," I said.

The baby shuffled around and cheeped every few seconds, ignoring the food at its feet. Still too young. The stunned adult blinked once. I wanted to finish up and go home. I went and found the tongs I use to poke mouse parts into the chick.

"Look!" the woman hissed.

The adult staggered forward and nearly fell on her face. When she straightened up, she had a mouse hind quarter in her beak. The baby cheeped. She pivoted slow and careful, one wing stuck out to keep her from falling over, and bumped the baby's beak with her own. The kid got it right–grabbed dinner and head-bobbed it right down. It shut up and the adult shut off, frozen in place.

"Wow," I said. "See? That cheep gets right through the fog. Gotta feed the baby."

"Wait till she wakes up and figures out it's not her kid," the woman said. "It'll be a different story then."

This little miracle was bogus? "Bull*shit*. It's a *baby*, it makes baby noises. She'll bust a gut trying to raise it."

They both looked at me the way you'd look at a dog that growled at you for no reason.

But she didn't back off. "Really?" Looking me in the eye. "They always will?"

I nodded and left it at that. Nothing is ever "always." Someone else could let her know.

The woman straightened up and moved away from me and him and the owls.

He watched while I fed the chick a few more pieces and gave the adult some glucose solution with a syringe. I got over my mad. Just weary in body and heart.

The woman looked in each cage. She didn't put her face close so I didn't have to snap at her. That heron would stab her in the eye in a heartbeat. I set the wire lid on the owl cage and said, "Folks, that's about it. It's a long way to Medford."

"Yeah," he said. "We got to get going."

The woman was across the room, staring at the windows, at her own reflection. Dark now outside. She pulled her shoulders back and took a heavy breath. Turned and looked at her man straight on. "Sacramento," she said. "We are going to Sacramento."

The man went still. Surprised and wary. A pause. "You're sure?"

"Yeah." She looked tired and determined and resigned. "Sacramento," and walked toward the door.

He reached toward her, careful, and she let him put an arm around her waist.

They thanked me and walked out, her leaning into him. I stood at the open door and watched the beater Toyota Corolla pull away.

I'd been wrong. She wouldn't be leaving him any time soon. I'd read my own troubles into them. She wouldn't quit on him, not yet at least. Not like Kate had quit on me. I almost envied them their troubles.

The heron hadn't puked. I took my time finishing up, then locked the door and walked outside into the night. The air was sweet with firs and soft from the creek. A bat flickered around the security light in the parking lot.

That weary couple should be about to Roseburg, some 400 miles left to go. I thought about what they expected in Sacramento that wasn't to be found in Medford and wished them more luck than they were used to.

# Dylan

Three in the afternoon, a rap on the window of my office door pulled me out of an email thread on calcium in baby hawk diets. Apparently Connie and her Receptionist sign wouldn't do. Whatever the problem was, it required a man in an office, the Director of the Lucille Whittaker Wildlife Clinic himself. I looked up from the computer and nodded. A round old guy opened the door. "Help you?" I said.

"Gotta a couple of blacktail fawns in the truck. I found them this morning. I hear you'll raise them." A farmer, maybe. Pink cheeks, pink scalp, faded blue jeans and a puffy blue jacket.

I stood up. "Sure. Where were they?" Usually the best thing for fawns is to put them back where they came from, where Mom is hiding in the bushes wondering what the hell happened to her babies.

"They were in a ditch on the side of the road. The doe was roadkill. She was cold, been there awhile. They were curled up next to her."

"Dylan," I called toward the back. Dylan was ignorant, but he ought to be able to hold a fawn, and the other volunteer, Janie, was in the middle of feeding baby birds.

He slipped by the reception desk and walked over, eyes wary, scanning the stranger.

"Come give me a hand. Fawns."

He relaxed, said, "At least it's not more *birds,*" and we trooped outside. Connie at the reception desk curled her upper lip in a sneer. She didn't like Dylan and she didn't like the farmer ignoring her and going to my office. "Oh, it's *men's* business," I read in her face. Middle-aged, childless, and trapped in a wheelchair, Connie suffered lots of fools politely, but never gladly. I took care to neither ignore nor acknowledge her sense of ownership toward the center.

I thought about fawns loose in the back of a truck and didn't like my conclusions. I liked them even less when he opened the flap of the canopy. It was hard to believe two fawns would fit in amongst the shovels, rakes, step ladders, and junk heaped in there. I revised my estimate from two broken legs to six. This was a death trap for panicky fawns thrashing around.

But they weren't thrashing. They were curled up exactly where he'd put them, each nestled in a coil of hose, too weak to raise their heads. Brown eyes stared at me, uncaring. The farmer lowered the tailgate and I lifted one out, feather-light. Ribby and limp. I handed it to Dylan and picked up the other one. "Jesus," I said, "they must have been out there for days." They looked to be about a week old. "We'll do what we can with them. Come fill out the intake form."

The center has the permits to rehab a few fawns each year. Fish and Wildlife picks them up when they're weaned. They turn them out into a non-hunting area to give them a chance to get wild.

Connie managed the farmer and the intake forms. Dylan held the fawns while I set up our biggest indoor cage for them. I put them on towels and sent him after two bottles of warm glucose solution. I could hear Janie minding him—"Not those nipples. Not too hot." He brought the bottles and I sat with them, holding their heads up, and got a little fluid down both. Not much sucking reflex. I covered the front of the cage with a blanket and left them in dim light to rest and warm up.

The farmer had gone and Dylan was idling in the kitchen. A scrawny kid, eighteen, lank brown hair and secretive dark eyes. Not bad looking, but I couldn't see what it was about him that got through to my ex-girlfriend Kate. She was a social worker connected to the courts and that was why Dylan was paying his debt to society at the rehab center, Kate asking me for a favor. Stunned by finding her on the other end of the phone, I'd have agreed to anything. A connection again, a tendril. So I'd said "Sure."

Dylan had a hundred hours to serve on a DUII, fourteen of them behind us. He had to be watched. At first, he'd been unwilling or unable to follow any procedure more complicated than filling a water bowl. He didn't seem stupid, though, and was picking up speed. Or so I'd hoped. I told him the floor needed mopping and knew Janie would see he did it right.

I was back in my office working when she came in without knocking and laid a dead baby robin on my desk, her face thunderous. Curly dark hair, shapely in a black Leonard Cohen tee shirt. Her paying job was as an oncology nurse. She said the rehab center kept her sane, and she was totally competent and as reliable as the sun.

"What?" I asked. We had two re-purposed aquariums full of orphaned baby robins. Now and then one dies. It happens.

"Look at it."

The nestling's mouth was open and full of the soft diet we prepare for them. Way too full. "Suffocated," I said, and sighed. "Dylan."

"It was in the garbage under some newspapers. I found it by accident." She gave me a heartbeat or two to speak, then, "How long do we have to put up with this? I know he's your special project, some guy mentor thing, but he's an idiot."

"I'll talk to him."

She waited to see if I had anything more. I didn't.

"You're the boss, Mister." Her hips twitched as she left. Janie flirted now and then, but this was all anger.

"*Dylan*," I yelled.

He came in and saw the robin right away. I watched him figure it out, but he was smart enough not to say anything.

"You overfed it," I said.

He took a step back. "They were all fine. I did it just like you showed me. Maybe Janie fed them again, maybe she didn't know I already had. But I told her I had. I don't know anything about this."

"It had to be you or Janie, and it wasn't Janie. It died and you hid it." I stood up to shut off his drivel and he backed further away, real fear in his eyes. I blew out a breath. This kid expected to be whapped around when he screwed up, and he was a lot smaller than I am. "Listen. You made a mistake. Everybody makes mistakes. Learn from it." I handed him the limp little body. "Wrap it up and put it where it belongs, in the freezer. And don't lie to me again or you are out of here for good."

Color rose on his cheeks and his lips thinned. He said, "It's just a lousy robin," took the bird, a wing-tip between finger tips, and walked back to the kitchen. Connie scowled at me from behind the reception desk.

I worked for a solid hour on the fundraising letter that might pay the center's utility bills and my salary for next few months. Janie and Dylan fed and cleaned and fed again. This was just the beginning of our busy season. Two people could handle it, no sweat, and have time for chit-chat and sharing cookies. Hearing the volunteers laugh always warmed me, although they usually stopped when I came near, as though I might think they weren't taking the work seriously. No laughter today. I left my door open and, when the washing machine quit its banging, I could hear. Janie and Dylan worked in silence.

I tried feeding the fawns again before I left for the day. One of them raised its head when I pulled the flap back and suckled with a hint of enthusiasm. I rubbed its butt to get it to pee, using a washcloth to duplicate the mother's tongue, but no luck. Still dehydrated. The other fawn fought the nipple, but sucked once it was in place. I hoped these were hints they could recover their place in the world of the living.

The fawns were both female. I found a felt marker and dabbed a green spot on the white ring around one's nose so I could tell them apart.

The next morning, I lifted the flap with a nervous heart. Surprise—both still alive. They fumbled to their feet and staggered away from me. I held the plain-nose one in the crook of my elbow and pried open her mouth to insert a nipple. Hunger took over and she forgot how scary I was. I stuck with the sugar water, but the next feeding could be dilute formula. Definitely looking better. The green-nose fawn was also stronger.

Connie wheeled in at 7:30 AM on the dot, as always, five days a week. She deserved a salary, but when I apologized for the lack of it, she said no way, it would only screw up her disability payments. "That jerk going to be here again?" she demanded.

Way to start the day. "He's supposed to be here three days a week. Today's one of them."

"When are you going to give up on him?"

"When you going to give him a chance?"

She didn't say anything.

I added, "Think 'foster care.' Think 'kicked out at eighteen.' Think 'never caught a break.'" Kate's words. "*Okay?*"

"Okay," Connie muttered. "I get why you're doing this."

I ignored the last part and Dylan showed up twenty minutes late.

"Cut that out," I said. "Get here on time."

He whined about the bus.

"Feed robins," I said, "and change the towels under them. Then the mallards. Come get me if you have any questions." I watched him slouch toward the back room. I'd been kicked out at eighteen, too. Had I been that hostile and incompetent?

Renee, another of the day's volunteers, was late too, but she'd warned me about her naturopath's appointment. She skipped in at ten AM, as promised. She was twenty-one, looked sixteen, and radiated conviction that the world was a benign and lovely place. She was vegan, of course, and confident that wearing a certain crystal would guarantee her anything she really wanted. In addition to her welcome sunshine, Renee was a blond, blue-eyed looker. I'd met her boyfriend, a dim and earnest yoga instructor, and wondered what he'd done to deserve her. He probably wondered, too.

"What's new?" she chirped.

Connie filled her in about a couple of baby wild rabbits that were recent arrivals. The concussed owl had its wits back, but we were holding it until its adopted chick was older. The green heron was eating on its own and had been moved outside. And we had fawns.

"Oooh. Can I see them? Please, please?"

I showed her the fawns and listened to her exclaim with joy and amazement, hands clasped to her admirable chest. "They are just *adorable.*" The fawns insisted they were invisible, tiny black hooves curled to their bellies, noses flat to the ground. They didn't need the stress of visitors, but this is the coin with which I pay my volunteers.

I sat in my office and re-read the fundraising letter, wishing yet again that some multi-millionaire would set up an endowment for the center so I would never have to beg again. The letter was as good as it was going to get, so I printed it for Connie to proofread before I sent it out. I started pawing through emails. I could hear the work on the other side of the center, Renee trilling and Dylan wise-cracking. Connie kept her eyes down.

I took a break and inspected the robins. "Good job, Dylan," I said, since they were all alive and lively.

"I cleaned them up. They had food all over themselves," Renee said, oblivious to tarnishing Dylan's gold star.

I pretended not to hear her and sent them out back to clean the flight cages.

The fawns had picked up strength and they each peed, finally. They didn't get it yet that me and my bottles were the new mom, but they didn't fight as hard as they could have. I felt pretty good about fetching them back from the brink of death, a human apology for killing their mother. Wildlife rehabilitation: our tiny sincere apology for wrecking everything.

Dylan came back in, flushed and smiling. "Edgar landed on my hand! He just hopped on over. He likes me!"

This was the first time I'd seen a smile on that closed, untrusting face. It looked good on him. Maybe Kate was on to something and this kid had a future in the non-loser world. Maybe Edgar Allen Crow saw the same thing. I said, "In a few weeks, you could start learning how to handle him for school shows."

"Why not now?"

"Because you need thirty hours of experience here before you get to work with the education birds." Dylan's face said this was stupid, but his mouth kept quiet.

A rush of animals came in throughout the morning, one cardboard box after another. A raccoon hit by a car, DOA. A clutch of scrub jays from a tree trimming project that took out their nest. A peeping downy mallard found alone at a park. Connie dealt with the people, Renee and Dylan incorporated the living newbies into the cages, and I sweet-talked a printer over the phone into donating another three hundred copies of our brochure.

I was in my office gnawing on leftover pizza when Connie hissed at me, "Get over here."

I came to her desk. "What?"

She jerked her head toward the kitchen behind her. I took a few steps and saw that Dylan had Renee herded into a corner, her back to the counter. Renee was engaged in describing the spiritual lessons she had learned from animals here at the center and how these had pulled her out of a really, really bad time and brought her closer to the Great Spirit that runs through all living creatures. Her blue eyes were intense, her hands waved in little circles for emphasis, and Dylan was hearing not a word. He was riveted on her, possibly not breathing.

"He's been stalking her all morning," Connie said.

They sure as hell weren't getting any work done.

"*Dylan,*" I said, and he spun toward me, fists up. "Outside."

I walked out to the parking lot and waited, keeping my hands loose at my sides. He hung back on the porch. His eyes flicked for exit routes. What would Kate say to him? I did not know. "Get this straight. You're not here to make time with Renee."

"I didn't do anything."

"No, but you were trying. This isn't the place."

"What, they're all yours? Or just her? Tell me how this works." Angry words from a boy not much more than half my size, half my age.

"Renee has a boyfriend. You're wasting your time, and she won't like it."

"I didn't *do* anything."

"Cut it out or leave and don't come back."

He rocked on his heels and looked at me, nodding. I could see it in his face–jerk, asshole. I gave him time to get to the next step. Sullen, he turned back inside. I followed.

Renee had been watching us through the window, bewildered. "Not your fault, honey," Connie said.

Dylan looked like he wanted to hit her, wheelchair or not.

The next day, the fawns were wheezy and weak and our vet, Dr. Hanson, put them on an antibiotic. Pneumonia. No big surprise. They ate pretty well. It's never over till it's over.

When Connie wheeled herself into the bathroom, I looked up from my desk and spotted Dylan lurking at the reception counter. He saw me watching and withdrew back into the kitchen. I didn't notice anything in his hands, but I got up and walked across the room to have a look. Her big purse leaned against the wall, unzipped. I stared hard at Dylan, who did a bad job of looking innocent and puzzled. "What? I was just looking for a pencil. In the desk."

"Don't ever look there again," I said.

Four days with no Dylan scheduled and then he was back, on time for once. Connie said "hi" to him in a voice that was almost friendly. Janie arrived in a Waylon Jennings tee shirt. She sucked it up and was pleasant to Dylan, too. No friction I could hear, no baby birds choking on their food, and—for sure—nothing physical. Janie would have cut out his liver with a paring knife.

The green-nose fawn was not perking up, but she ate. The plain-nose fawn was stronger and ready for bigger quarters. I decided not to separate them and left them where they were.

Dylan was eager to clean the flight cages, and I sent Janie with him. Again he came in smiling about the crow flying to him. Janie shook her head at him, but she smiled, too. Maybe the animals could work some magic on Dylan– he wouldn't be the first. Neither of us mentioned that Edgar lived a captive life because he was imprinted on people. He hopped on most of the volunteers.

Janie left at noon and the afternoon volunteer called in sick. Dylan did the afternoon feedings alone. I sent him outside with the garbage bags and did a quick inspection. The baby robins looked good–fed and clean. But the baby raccoons were sticky and when I rubbed their butts, they peed and pooped copiously. He'd forgotten to do it. He'd peeked at the fawns, too, rearranging their blanket, ignoring the Do Not Disturb sign.

When Dylan came back in, I told him to clean up the raccoons and watched him do it. At least he didn't complain. I felt Connie's eyes on us. When he'd done the dishes and laundry, I told him we were in pretty good shape and gave him some kibble to hand-feed to Edgar.

After half an hour, I checked through the back window. He wasn't in the crow cage. The door to the great horned owl cage was open, but I didn't see him. I went out there and, sure enough, he was in the owl's shed. He'd gotten Hooter onto his bare wrist and was trying to get him to eat bits of kibble. I stepped back and kept quiet to keep from startling the bird. Dylan didn't notice me.

I waited and, when he didn't come out, walked to the porch and called him. He came in with a guilty shine to him. "Did you remember to latch Hooter's door?" I asked.

"I never opened it." He said it fast, a reflex.

I kept some of the snarl out of my voice, not all. "Did you forget what I told you about going in with any bird but the crow? Did you forget what I said about a great horned's talons? If that bird grabbed you, we might have to kill him to get him off. You risked his life, not just your arm."

He see-sawed between anger and denial. "I didn't hurt anything. He likes me."

"He's old and tame, and you were lucky. Don't ever break a rule like that again." It sounded weak as I said it, and I could tell he heard it that way. "Get out of here. And just so you know, owls won't eat kibble."

He took off for his bus and I went out and checked the birds' doors. They were latched. I watched Edgar hop around and waited for the anger to trickle out. Maybe I did need to punch that kid. Maybe that was the only way he could learn anything. My fingers bunched and I hated the anger and the nausea. I'd never been any good with people who insisted on their own desires and expected animals to accommodate them.

The next morning, the green-nose fawn was dead. When Connie rolled in, she saw the black garbage bag on the floor and understood the shape of it. "Oh, no. I thought she was going to make it."

"You can't save them all," I told her.

"That's a fact," she said. "That is truly a fact. But I gotta hand it to you for trying." She looked at me from her wheelchair, sad and wise.

I closed my office door and sat there for awhile, thinking about the busy season coming up, about the reliable, capable roster of volunteers I'd developed. In summer, I would be out of the center picking up and releasing birds, relying on them even more. I rubbed my face with my hands, thinking how good it must feel to pop some asshole a good one. As an antidote, I dredged up being eighteen and the people who had kept me from the worst of myself. I thought about the niche and solace this rehab center had given me when I was drifting, about relationship failures and rare opportunities to try again.

When I still ended up looking at my fists, I called Kate.

"I tried to make it work," I told her, "but I can't. Dylan's slow to learn, he won't listen to me, and he's hurting me with my volunteers. He's a safety risk for himself and the animals. I can't afford him, especially not when we get busier. Not for all the hours he's got left."

She changed to the voice that usually gets her whatever she wants from me. "I've seen this kid off and on for a couple of years now, and he looks better than he ever did. He loves it. Told me all about the crow and the fawns. You're making a difference in his life, just like I hoped you would. Hang in there. He's really trying."

It had taken a lot out of me to make this call and now it wasn't done, wasn't over. I held the phone long enough for her to say, "You still there?"

I wasn't going to tell her about the anger, about wanting to pound on this damaged boy. "Kate, I can't have him here and get the job done."

"Birds and bunnies or this kid's future? I think you can turn this kid around, I really do."

"Kate. I tried. I can't do this, even for you."

She sat on the line for a few seconds. "Okay, then." Brisk. "Don't say anything to him. I'll take care of it." She hung up. Maybe she could cook up a story to spare the kid's pride.

I felt like I'd run a marathon and then been beaten with sticks. She did this stuff every single working day. Would she give me any points for trying? Didn't sound like it.

I told Connie I'd be out for an hour. Walking a steep trail, spotting deer tracks, and listening to the towhees and song sparrows sent me back slightly less roiled. I boxed up a screech owl and the green heron for release, always the best part of the job and maybe a remedy for the pain of failure.

Dylan didn't come in the next day. But he came in that night—smashed a window, trashed my office, took the keys from the reception desk drawer, and opened all the cages for the education birds.

The owl didn't want to go anywhere, and the hawk couldn't fly, and nothing got in to eat them, so that was all right. Edgar was gone. I thought Dylan had stolen him, but he landed on my head that afternoon during my lunch walk along the creek. I took him back to his home. My office needed tidying anyway.

Dylan's hurt and rage weren't as easy to put behind me.

Or Kate's disappointment.

The farmer dropped by a few days later to find out what happened to the fawns. I showed him the survivor and told him I thought this one would make it.

# Release to the Wild

"It's my weasel and I am taking it home," Willard Jeckel informed me as I stepped out of the back room and in front of Connie and her reception desk. His voice was a gravel rumble and his face was grim. A thin line of facial hair circled his lips, marking a muzzle. He was a big man in a tight tee-shirt, jeans, and motorcycle boots, who gave every sign that he took weight-lifting seriously. He hadn't come alone. His buddy was equally large and dressed similarly, but had his face arranged in more of a sneer. They weren't young—fifties, maybe—and they showed hard use.

"Not happening," Connie said. "That's a wild animal and it belongs in the wild."

She seems to think her wheelchair came equipped with a military-grade force field. Willard and Co. ignored her now that I'd shown up—forget the gray-haired woman and talk to the bearded guy. I'd hear about it from Connie later.

"What's up?" I asked, knowing pretty well what was. Willard T. Jeckel had enough troubles that I was surprised he bothered with his pet weasel. I'd learned his name and charges days ago from the cop who dropped off a five-gallon bucket with a young weasel in it. A loud party had escalated to an arrest—felon in possession of guns and heroin. Yet he made bail.

I wanted to know—*really* wanted to know—who decided to tell Willard that his confiscated pet had been delivered to the Lucille Whittaker Wildlife Clinic.

I'd been in back getting some new bunnies settled in when I heard Connie arguing with these lunkheads. It was early in the day, just the two of us on duty. The rabbits were a damn nuisance, domestics abandoned on our front porch. We raised the native species now and then, but these were big juveniles blotched in black and white. Wild rabbits—little brown ones—would have been comatose with terror, praying for a chance to bolt before they were eaten alive. This pair was disconcerted, but still managed to stuff in the hay I'd provided. Floppy ears. Cute. We don't do domestics. We have more than enough business with the wild animals that run afoul of our species. Kate might have a friend who'd want them, but using that as an excuse to call her would be pathetic.

"I'm not leaving without my property," Willard said. "Where's it at?"

"Wild animals are *not* private property," Connie said. "There's *laws*."

I put a hand on her shoulder. "I've got this."

She looked like she doubted that very much. Usually she gives me a pass for being the wrong gender, but there are times.

"How'd you ever get a weasel?" I asked with genuine curiosity. It arrived tame enough to handle, a fine little thing. Felt like velvet over mercury, slippery and soft and intense.

Willard studied me. Size matters in confrontations for most species, and I wasn't any smaller than he was. He had me on weight, I had height.

"Friend of mine found it," he grated.

"Unusual to see them."

"One was in his wood pile. He clobbered it with a piece of stove wood."

Connie flinched and scrunched up her face.

Willard glanced at her. "Jake's a moron." He said it like it was a diagnosis. "Then he found the nest. One of the babies got crushed, but he kept the other. I bought it off him for my old lady."

I nodded. "How long did you have it?"

"Couple a weeks. She wants it bad. It's back there?"

I shook my head.

Two volunteers, Renee and Fred, would be in soon. Not good to have them walk into this, and no magic words were coming to me to get rid of these guys. "She's in a cage outside. We're training her for release, feeding live mice. She bit her first mouse in the back of the skull like a pro. They're instinctual killers."

"She?"

"Female."

"Huh. They're supposed to be real mean suckers, but it never bit anyone."

His friend shifted his weight, bored.

I said, "It's young. Anything is nice until it grows up. Then they don't want us bothering them."

He considered the implications of that bit of wisdom and moved on. "It's going with me. We don't want any trouble." He rocked his shoulders side to side, making it clear that there could, indeed, be trouble.

Connie had too much time to think. She turned to me. "Don't do them like you did the guy who kicked his dog in front of you. I don't want to have to see that again ever."

I blinked. "Um, two nights in the hospital and he was fine. Nothing like that's going to happen."

Willard narrowed his eyes at me. "Military?"

"Tae kwon do. Black belt." For modesty, I added, "A while ago."

"Karate and kick boxing," said Willard. *His* credentials.

His buddy snorted. "Is that what you call it, Py? We call it ca-*tas*-tro-phe. With a side of mayhem."

Decent vocabulary.

"Py?" I asked.

"Pyro," said Willard.

A relief. Nobody deserves "Willard."

His buddy stared hard at me, nodding slowly as if he had my number. He was putting serious effort into intimidation, and it was working well. A scar wound across his buzz-cut scalp and the inevitable tattoo on his left cheek was a human skull.

All this fuss for a quarter-pound of *Mustela frenata*.

I wanted them out of the building now, before Renee and Fred showed up. "Let's go outside and take a look. I haven't fed her yet." I went into the back room and came out with a Folger's can with the lid on. I lifted it. "Mouse."

Pyro cocked an eye at me and then the can, a look that I took to mean, "Better be just that."

Connie cut a glance at the phone.

"Nash, you stay here," Pyro said.

I was cheered at having to deal with only one of them, until I deduced that Pyro was confident he could handle me alone.

We walked around the building to the back and then a ways into the woods where I had a hardware-cloth cage set up for squirrels. The squirrels we had now were too young to go outside, so it was available. It was pretty roomy, about three feet to a side, and had branches and a nest box up high. A place to get used to the scents and temperature of the woods and to be away from people. I liked it there myself.

"Didn't finish dinner," I said, pointing to a half-eaten mouse on the cage floor. "I'm not sure how much she needs, so I've been overfeeding." A nice firm scat lay near the carcass, thin and lumpy the way mustelid scats are. I could smell it, but mostly the firs and crisp morning air.

Pyro walked around the cage. "I got a friend could build one of these, in case it gets mean." He stopped and looked at me, his lumpy face shrewd. "I know that was bullshit about you and tae kwon do. That cripple lady is full of crap. You probably never been in a real fight your whole life. Just tell her I made it worth your while."

He had called it. I hadn't been in a fight since middle school. Even the guys my size didn't want to try me, not after that first one. I shook my head. "I could surprise you." That was lame. "Look." I pointed out the little weasel face in the nest box's round opening. Beady eyes watched us and whiskers twitched.

For lack of a better idea, I dumped the mouse inside and closed the little door. The mouse sniffed around, wondering where he'd landed. The weasel flowed out of the box and onto a branch above it. She was a beautiful thing—brown on top with a yellow belly and throat, a black tip on the tail. Not hungry, I guessed, or she would have attacked immediately.

Then another mouse shot out of nowhere and jumped the new mouse. Identical brown blurs, the two whirled and squeaked and fought like miniature wolves. The weasel went nuts, jumping around in a frenzy, lunging at them. Every hair on her tail was erect and she gave shrill little barks. The mice separated and the weasel was on one of them in an instant. She gave it a sniff and whirled onto the other, sniffed it, and killed it in an eye blink.

I was speechless.

Pyro said, "Awesome! She's greased lightning."

"Replay that," I said. "This makes no sense."

The weasel hauled the freshly dead mouse around for a minute or two, then put it down and climbed back into the nest box. The surviving mouse followed. Two little faces peered at us out of the opening.

"Do you get that?" I said, close to incoherent. "Did you *see* that? This god-damned weasel has a *pet mouse*. It killed the *new* one. *Damn!*" I turned to him. "You are my witness. No one would ever believe this."

Pyro was wide-eyed. "Cool. This is totally cool."

I paced around, rattled. "Holy crap. Don't ever tell anybody or we'll both be in the looney bin."

Pyro grinned. "Some weasel, huh?"

"Some *mouse*."

We watched the mouse clean his whiskers. The weasel hid inside.

"Why'd that one mouse fight the other?" Pyro asked.

"Territory. Must be the same gender." I pulled myself back to the problem at hand. "Look, this weasel was gentle because she was just a kid. But now she's growing up and she doesn't want to be your buddy. She wants to run around and kill things and find a big stud weasel and make baby weasels. We've got a great release site, a goat dairy with a bad mouse problem." I stopped and thought. "And I'm going to see that this mouse gets released with her. It earned that."

Pyro shook his head and resumed his scowl. "No can do. It's going with me. I'll do right by it, so don't you worry." He reached for the cage door. I clamped a hand on his wrist, knowing it was the wrong thing to do.

"You really want to do it this way?" Pyro asked, the harsh voice gone mild.

"It's my job." I let go and stood back. The scar on the heel of my right palm itched.

He hesitated, brow wrinkling in puzzlement, one big hand still on the cage door latch. "Why do you care? If you're just gonna turn it loose anyway."

I shrugged, feeling how tight my shoulders were. "She should be wild. This is her chance to get back on track. It's what we do."

His mouth quirked sideways. "If it was just me, maybe. But my old lady, she's expecting it back. She's been in a bad patch, and playing with it made her smile. Can't disappoint her, y'know?" He turned to face me—no mistaking his intention—and my heart started thudding. I was twelve again, Bobby Fitz falling back stunned, his mouth red and dark where it shouldn't have been. His front teeth embedded in my palm. A fight he started, over with a single shove–the big kid clobbered the little kid. And all the adults had come unglued. Threats of law suits, dental bills, "counseling." It had gone on forever.

Pyro had decades of experience brawling, and I'd done all I could to evade those lessons. My own course of study worked pretty well, but not today.

One more try. "Women usually understand about things growing up and leading their own lives." I had no idea if this was true.

But it hit the wrong nerve. "Bull*shit*." He looked like he wanted to pop me for reasons having nothing to do with any animal.

He didn't know or care anything about my clinic and what it did, and he wasn't going to learn. He just came to take what he wanted. No words would get us out of this. It was pretty simple, really.

All the times I'd been polite to fools and strategic toward people who just didn't care, all the frustrations over funding and regulations or the lack of them, all my failures with the person I most cared about—the lid I kept on the dark mess slipped sideways. A deranged outlaw glee flooded my veins. I was ready, too.

He jerked on the door latch and I shoved him. He swung at my face. I ducked and it skidded off, but the next one landed on my cheek and stopped my brain. I lurched back, breathing hard, arms up, and Pyro paused to see if that was enough. He was focused, ready. He knew how to do this. He was going to hit me until I stopped hitting back, and then he was going to take the weasel.

"Hey." A small voice startled us. Fred, the volunteer. We hadn't heard him come up. Pyro glanced toward him, just a flicker, but his timing was bad. My fist hitting his chin jolted all the way up to my shoulder. Pyro swung around and dropped flat.

Wow.

I stood holding my aching hand while Fred stared at me open-mouthed. Pyro rolled to his knees and stood up. I glimpsed his buddy on the trail, looking for us.

"You're cut," Fred said. I thought he meant Pyro. Then I saw drops bright against the forest duff by my boots. Probably my cheekbone where I'd been clocked. Big deal. I'd seen blood before. I'd also seen the movies and TV shows and knew what I was supposed to do: knee Pyro in the face, punch him in the gut, keep hammering. But the rage had already ebbed.

Pyro hunched his shoulders and took a step toward me.

His wingman sauntered up, grinning. "He had enough yet?"

Pyro seemed to figure out at the same time I did that Nash hadn't seen him go down. He just saw the blood dripping off my beard. Good. This would never be over if Py had even more face at stake.

Fred was a little squirt. The only way he'd be any use in a fight was if he'd brought a baseball bat, which he hadn't.

Damn. Renee was trotting up the trail, blond hair swinging, all hundred and ten pounds of her. This was getting complicated. She stopped several yards away and looked over the scene. "This is way too primal," she said. "Connie is calling the cops. You-all need to inhale some forest essence and chill out." She wasn't smart-mouthing. Renee believed aromas changed people's brain chemistry.

"I've got my phone," Fred said. He kept well back, waving the phone's face at us with a shaking hand.

Took me a second to get it. He meant he would take pictures. Evidence.

The anger finished draining, leaving a tired, sour stain. The equation had changed—Pyro was hesitating, recalculating. He and his buddy could pound me senseless, shove Fred and Renee out of the way, and take the weasel, but that now had a price. Assault charges, for openers. But I couldn't let them retreat just to come back at night, steal the weasel, and torch my clinic.

Surely all those years of deflecting my own anger had taught me something useful.

"Pyro," I said, with no idea what was going to come out of my mouth, "this lady of yours. She must be a strong woman, to be with a guy like you, right?"

No response from that iron face, but his buddy nodded, looking like he was also wondering where this was going.

"But she's got a softer side, too." Nothing from either. "This weasel's a pretty thing, but she's gone wild now. You saw that. She can't go back to being a pet, any more than you or I could hold down a desk job." Excellent—my brain wasn't wrecked. "But I think there's another way to make your lady happy." I stopped breathing and watched Pyro scowl and finish his math.

Maybe twenty minutes later, the squad car arrived, flashing red and blue. Pyro was climbing into his huge black Sierra truck. Nash was on the passenger side with a big cardboard box on his lap. The cop parked crosswise to block the exit from the parking lot, and two officers got out and walked to the truck. I left the porch and joined them, holding a paper towel to my face. "I think we're OK now," I said. "We settled our problem. Right?"

Pyro nodded.

I waited for more, holding up a hand to keep the cops at bay for a second.

His scowl deepened. "Don't push it, mouse."

I let him have that and stepped back.

There was more hassle than just that, but in the end, the truck and the squad car left. I washed the blood off. Renee found a bandage and drew two butterflies on it, one yellow, one green, before sticking it over my cut. Fred went into the back room and sat on the floor for ten minutes. Connie reamed me out for not pressing charges and fixed up an ice bucket for my hand.

It took some doing to get people back to feeding baby birds and answering the phone. I sat in my office alone for a few minutes, soaking my hand, waiting to see whether the old fear and shame about losing my temper would bubble up. This time it didn't. I'd hit a guy as hard as I could, and he wasn't dead or broken.

When my hand was willing to work again, I cleaned the empty cage where the domestic rabbits had been. Smiling hurt, so I tried to quit doing it.

# Trying to Help

The white dog trotting in the road glanced over his shoulder at my car, but didn't yield the lane. It was early in the morning, half a mile from the clinic, with hardly any traffic. Stop and try to catch him and pack him off to the pound? Or go around and leave him to his own business? I'd spotted a place to pull over when he loped off into the bushes alongside the road. He looked like he knew what he was doing. Heading home, maybe, after a night of adventures.

The day would be hot, again. Summer had come on early and hard. The overhanging fir trees that made the Lucille Whitaker Wildlife Center cold and dank in winter made up, a little, for the lack of air conditioning. I started the fans and opened all the windows.

I'd fed maybe half of the baby birds and juvenile squirrels by the time Janie, the very best of my volunteers, arrived. She helped me finish and then lit into cleaning with fierce concentration, normal for the first part of her shift. I'd learned to stay out of her way until the cages and kitchen met her standards. Then she'd be sociable. Today's tee shirt was blue, Rolling Stones. I could relax a little during Janie's shift.

Other volunteers arrived and had settled into cleaning and feeding by the time the first citizen with a wildlife problem drove in.

A gasping scrub jay fluttering in her hand, the heavy-set woman explained to me why it wasn't her cat's fault. "I mean, Mister, I know it's natural, but I couldn't stand to watch the bird suffer, so I took it away from my cat. It's not hurt very bad."

No, it wasn't her cat's fault. It was her fault, and the bird would die. "We get hundreds of birds every year that cats have caught. They almost all die. You can read the evidence here." I handed her the cat brochure. "Your cat will be healthier if you keep it indoors." The standard message, with the standard reply—

"She hates being inside. I can't keep her penned up in the house all the time. She hardly ever bothers the birds." Her round face was earnest. Brown curls bobbed with conviction.

I was fed up long ago with arguing about free-roaming cats. Connie, our receptionist, was way better at this. She still liked cats. Connie was off today and the sooner I ended this, the better. I handed the woman an intake form and put the jay in a box to die in peace. It was a juvenile, feathers not yet fully developed. Its eyes were already glazing over.

A call came in to pick up three sick mallards from a pond on a golf course. Could be pesticide poisoning or, more likely, botulism from overcrowding. No rain for weeks and the water level was low everywhere. When I got back, I called our vet, got instructions, and set up the half-paralyzed ducks. No water bowl, to keep the incapacitated birds from drowning themselves. Janie's shift was done—noon—and she was logging out on the clipboard in the reception area. A quiet time for me to eat a sandwich and read email.

But she stuck her head into my office. "Hey," she said, "I forgot to tell you. I met your friend Kate. Kate Alvarez."

"Uh," I said. "How'd that happen?"

"At work."

A moment of panic. Kate in Janie's oncology clinic... "She's okay?"

Janie needed a beat. "Oh. No. It's a kid she's working with. Leukemia. Kate's fine. The kid will be okay, too." She paused. "We got to talking in the waiting room."

Kate and I had met over three Canadian geese goslings she'd found wandering in a city park. We had paired up for a few months, and I'd thought it would be permanent. But

Kate gave up on me and moved on. She said that being with me made her lonely.

"I mentioned working here and she asked about you."

The implications cascaded in an icy deluge. Kate the social worker and Janie the chemotherapy nurse dissecting me.

I said, "Glad she's not sick. Did you remember to empty the garbage under the sink? It was really stinking." Lame.

Janie smiled, tolerant. "I emptied it. Turns out she's a neighbor. Two blocks down. I'll see you next week."

"Have a good afternoon," I said, unreasonably relieved. Because Kate was all right and had asked about me or because Janie was dropping the subject? I couldn't say.

Janie opened the front door and stepped out. And stepped back. "Hey. We're having a few friends over on Sunday. Why don't you drop by? It's just pizza and beer. Seven o'clock."

"Uh. Sure. I guess so."

"You've got my address. See you Sunday." With a smile, she left for real.

Shit.

The next week was busy, normal for summer. The white dog showed up and hung around. Whippy tail, thin coat, pit-bull head. Thin. No collar. No home, I deduced. It ducked away into the woods surrounding the rehab center whenever I got close. I'd have to catch him before he got hungry enough to break into the squirrel enclosure or the mews where the owl and crow lived. I set out dog chow. Feed him, get him used to me, get a rope on him. Then haul him off to the pound and possibly a better fate. If he had a chip, maybe reunite him with his owner, although that seemed unlikely.

In the evenings after shutting down the clinic, I cozied up to the dog. Slow going, but after a few days, he would eat while I sat within five or six feet of him. I'd have to noose him with a catch pole if he wouldn't let me touch him. That wouldn't be pretty–he was big enough to put up a stiff fight. Maybe I could rent a good-sized live trap and try that.

Janie came in on Monday for her weekly shift and looked at me with reproach. "You missed a good party."

"Sorry. Something came up at the last minute."

She went on about the fun they'd had. "Oh, and I guess I should tell you. Kate's moving in a couple of days. She found a rental closer to downtown. She probably could use some help." She turned away into the kitchen and lit into scrubbing everything in sight, exactly as though she weren't meddling in my life.

After stewing about it all that night, I called Kate the next day and offered to help. She sounded flustered and rattled on about the new place (closer to work, more space) and that she'd rented a truck and her brothers would help move her stuff. Finally she said yes, another body would be great, and sounded as though she meant it. Saturday morning about ten would be good.

I'd been to her place before and had met one of her brothers. His van, with "Alvarez Concrete–Sidewalks Driveways" on the side, was parked out front with the doors all open. Kate looked disheveled in old jeans and a sagging sweatshirt. She zinged around scolding on her cell phone about the rental truck being late while scribbling labels on boxes stacked on the lawn. She cut off the call when she saw me, took a breath, and introduced me to the three brothers, who had paused on the porch and front steps with their arms full of boxes and chairs. They eyed me about like you would the local car prowler. I asked how I could help, and the one I'd met before, Ralph, said he thought they had it covered, but thanks for the offer. Kate fired off a blast of shrapnel in Spanish and the three men flinched.

Ralph said, "Well, Kate thinks we could use a hand with the fridge. We could go take a look." Kate explained that she'd bought her own fridge a year ago because the landlord wouldn't replace the broken one and that the stove didn't work very well either and the plumbing was a problem, too. She was tense and talked too fast. When she ran down, Ralph and I walked into the kitchen and looked at the fridge.

The two of us wrestled it out onto the lawn, the other brothers smart enough to keep out of the way. The rental truck had arrived. Ralph and I shoved the fridge onto the lift gate and horsed it in and to the rear. Kate had disappeared. Ralph assured me that they wouldn't have any trouble getting the fridge into Kate's new place. He thanked me and offered a beer. I took the hint and left.

Halfway back to the clinic, I was over being peeved and could appreciate the brothers' defensive circle around their sister. I'd never had the chance to play that role with my own sisters. Half-sisters. Their father didn't like me and didn't want me around once my mother died.

Kate had a real family, not just a thin genetic link to a few other people.

The Alvarez family didn't want me around either.

Kate called on her lunch hour the next day. "My brothers are only part-time assholes, honest. I never said a single word negative about you, but they make up their own stories. I'm really sorry they were jerks. It was good of you to help out." She talked on for a bit about the new place and said good-bye, see you later. It was an unsatisfactory conversation.

Sunday, the maintenance manager of the golf course showed up at the clinic with another dozen ducks–mallards, a green-winged teal, and two white domestics–all of them sick. While I was treating and housing them, Connie fielded a stream of people with young birds found on the ground, a squirrel hit by a car, and a dead and decaying Coopers hawk. The guy with the hawk had a vague idea that it had to be dealt with properly and not left to compost under the fir tree where he had found it.

Focusing on work instead of Kate was a relief, even if many of the day's intakes were not likely to survive.

I found reasons to be out of the office for Janie's next shift, but she tracked me down at the mews. I was reinforcing the wire on the crow enclosure so I could quit worrying about the white dog breaking in.

She chatted with the crow and handed me some nails. I waited for it. After a few minutes, she said, "Stan and I are kayaking on the Willamette next Saturday, with a couple of friends. We've got an extra kayak if you want to try it."

"Sure. I mean, I'll let you know." "A couple of friends" probably meant a woman she wanted me to meet. At my old job at the hardware store, a co-worker kept trying that. "We're tube feeding those sick ducks. There's instructions on the chart."

She tucked her chin to give me a look and walked to the back room. I didn't like the set of her shoulders.

I was still outside when a resounding metallic boom startled me and the crow. I quick-stepped toward the parking lot. A woman had driven her car slam-bang into the dump box, smacking it against a corner of the clinic. She staggered out of the black Lexus, older, thin, and bleeding freely from her face. Pale green shirt streaked with red, dark pants. "Help me. I need help. Please." She surely did.

I took her arm and got her to a chair in the reception area. The woman was sobbing, half-hysterical. Maybe entirely hysterical. Janie cleaned up her face with a damp towel, revealing vicious scratches that narrowly missed each eye. Janie said soothing words, including that we would get her to the hospital.

I said, "I'll go see that she turned off the car."

"No!" the woman said. "There's a bird inside. It attacked me. I was trying to help and it attacked me. It stabbed me. Over and over."

Janie said more soothing words.

I went out and took a look. A frantic heron loose in the car was trying to bash its way through the front passenger window. One wing hung useless. The bird whacked the window with the good wing and followed up with its heavy bill.

I opened the door and grabbed the black bill, then wrapped up the wings against my body. The gray and white bird struggled mightily, then gave up and went limp. I carried it inside, yellow legs dangling, turning so the woman didn't have to look at it, and put it in an animal carrier.

"What is it?" she asked, her voice dull.

"Black-crowned night heron. Long-billed birds go for the eyes when they're cornered."

"I saw it get hit by a car. I thought it would know I was trying to help."

Right. An injured bird can tell that a weird great ape grabbing at it, the same species that blasts ducks out of the sky, was trying to help.

"We'll get you to a doctor. Don't want that to scar," Janie said.

I told them the car had a dented bumper, but looked drivable. The dump box and the clinic didn't look too damaged either, but I didn't mention that. After some back-and-forthing, the woman agreed to let Janie drive her to the hospital in the Lexus. Janie could catch a bus home from there and Stan, her husband, would drive her back to the clinic to get her car. I offered to help, but they had it all worked out. The woman was calming down.

I drove the heron to the vet, who decided the wing could be saved and put a pin in it. It was late by the time I got back to the clinic, set up the heron, and closed down. After muscling the dumpster back where it belonged, I set out the bowl of dog food. The day was cooling down and getting dim. I took a seat on the bench in front of the clinic and thought about Janie and how much worse this morning's incident would have been if she hadn't been there.

The clinic couldn't survive without volunteers. They are mostly women, all of them peppered with uncharted landmines. Sometimes the IEDs explode in anger, sometimes I step into tears. After four years, I'm almost used to it.

The dog showed up and ate. I left it alone and went home to my cabin.

I met Stan for the first time the next morning when he dropped Janie off to get her car. She looked good in a red Eric Clapton tee shirt. He looked pretty good, too. Light-weight guy, built like a runner. We shook hands in the parking lot and said the usual things. I told him that Janie had been great with the injured woman and was a fine volunteer. He said, "She's fine in all sorts of ways," and looked me over and chewed his lower lip.

I tried to look harmless.

He gave Janie a good-bye kiss that lasted a beat longer than necessary and drove away.

Janie said that the woman probably wouldn't scar and wanted to know about the night heron.

"I gave it bait herring and mice," I told her, "and they all vanished. The wing'll take maybe six weeks to heal. If it keeps eating and doesn't bash around too much we should be able to release it."

"You could call that lady and let her watch. Maybe she'll feel better about the whole experience if she sees it put back in the wild. She was pretty freaked out."

"Sure." I'd think about it. Probably not.

"You'll come Saturday, right? We'll bring the extra kayak."

I said, "Um. Sure."

She described where and when to meet up at the river.

After closing down, I took my seat out front. I could hear the highway, but the smells were woods and creek and dust. Everything was dry, grass turning brown a month early.

Janie was my best volunteer and, until recently, she was fun to have around. Now she was plotting to improve my life. I hunched forward on the bench. No way could I mingle with a bunch of strangers. If I got mixed up in Janie's social life, it was bound to go wrong. Then she'd quit because I'd screwed up. "Crap. I don't need this."

The dog, stepping out of the bushes, stopped when I spoke. He watched me, pale against the dark foliage. Then, keeping a close eye on me, he walked to the bowl and scarfed the contents. I stood up, took a step toward him, and stopped when his head came up, careful not to spook him. A step closer each day and maybe he'd let me touch him or get a noose over his head.

"She's meddling," I told him. "Yeah, I'm a meddler, too. You need to find a better gig. You're never going to make it through the winter."

After another long look at me–is that all?– he disappeared into the woods.

He still wouldn't let me close to him when Janie's next shift came around. She wore a Kiss tee-shirt and a professional attitude. No chit-chat. Cleaned cages like a fury.

I cut up fish in the kitchen while she washed dishes and tried to loosen things up by updating her about the dog, "It's still hanging around. Ugliest thing you ever saw. I have to catch it before it gets run over or digs into a cage out back. I've put out food for days and it still won't let me near."

She banged a metal food bowl into the sink, turned to face me, and said, "We had to give up Saturday and go back home. We waited an hour because we couldn't just leave the spare kayak behind and go off and let it get stolen. You didn't answer the phone. I would have appreciated a call if you weren't coming."

After a little moment, I said, "I am truly sorry about that." Never crossed my mind that she really expected me to show up and that there might be complications if I didn't. I tried to think of what else to say and came up empty.

Janie scrubbed fiercely at ancient char on the outside of a pot. I put the fish into a food pan and took it to the heron.

I took my time. When I came back, I apologized again. She said, "Anyway, I want to try catching that dog. You aren't getting anywhere."

That evening, she came back to the clinic and sat on the bench outside. I busied myself inside, watching through the window now and then. The dog showed up on schedule. I figured he'd be put off by a stranger, but the food counted for more. After he'd eaten, Janie walked closer to him and squatted down, holding out her hand with more chow in it, talking to him.

And he trotted up to her, ate from her hand, and let her scratch his neck.

So much for my special way with animals.

She slipped a piece of clothesline over his head, scratched his spine by his tail, and led him into the clinic. "What a sweetie!" She looked triumphant and vindicated. The dog edged away from me, but changed his mind after a bit and let me pet him. We took turns hand-feeding him a lot more chow.

Janie handed me the rope. "You should keep him. Seriously. You need a dog." She shook her head at me and left us.

I scratched his bony back and his tail whipped around. Then he tucked his nose down and pressed his face against my knees, hiding his eyes like a blind puppy might, for just a second. He backed off and sat down to scratch his neck with a hind foot.

A dog was the last thing I needed. Couldn't leave him home alone all day. Couldn't have him at the clinic scaring everything and everyone. Didn't have time to train him. Couldn't afford the vet bills.

Kept him anyway.
A fair price to pay.

# Done Right

"What the hell?" Bad policy to swear in front of strangers and I rarely did. But this... "You could of waited a couple weeks for them to fledge before you tore all these nests down. It doesn't take that long." I'd come out to the clinic's parking lot to see what this guy was unloading. Four open-topped boxes full of ruined mud nests and bewildered or crippled baby barn swallows sat on the pavement. Most were little balls of pin feathers with bright yellow linings to their soft, wide beaks. Some were a few days older and covered with dark brown feathers on top, buff on their bellies.

The guy wore jeans and a green shirt and lace-up boots, like any local, but his looked new and expensive. He was almost as tall as me, but lighter built. Drove a big double-cab pickup with a shiny locking toolbox in the bed. "McGillvery's Construction–Jobs Done Right" was painted on the door.

"I said we could delay a week or two, but the owner wants her horse barn reroofed right now." He pulled his mirror shades down and looked me in the eye so I'd know he was telling the truth. "She told me to bring them here so the birds would be okay."

Really? You can smash living things and the wildlife clinic is supposed to make it all better? I started stacking the boxes to take in. "Aside from the fact that what you did is illegal, this is a lot of birds and a lot of work for us. We've got bills to pay and feed to buy. You going to make a donation to cover some of the costs?"

"Illegal?" That stopped him for a second. "Okay, I'll see about a check." He started to reach out a hand to shake, thought better of it, and turned toward his truck.

"Wait up. We need you to fill out the intake form so we know where to release them."

"I'm kind of in a rush right now. I'll drop by tomorrow and take care of it. And that donation." An apologetic smile and he was in the truck and gone.

McGillvery's Construction. I'd remember that. Son of a bitch.

I notified the authorities, but didn't expect a response. Barn swallows aren't endangered and they aren't game birds and they aren't flashy raptors. The contractor never showed up with that check, no surprise either.

When the babies were feathered out, about two weeks, I called McGillvery's Construction and talked to the young woman who answered. "I'm calling from the Whittaker Wildlife Clinic, the bird care center. Your boss dropped off the swallow nests he took down at the horse barn project, and now the babies are old enough to fly. We'll be happy to release them if you give me the address of the barn."

The girl dithered about what project it was and whether she could tell me the address.

I said, "We need to take them back where they came from or they won't survive." This wasn't particularly true, but I wanted to chat with the lady at the horse barn who had to have those nests knocked down in such a hurry.

The girl gave up the address. I got Fred, the volunteer on duty, to look it up on his phone and show me how to get there. Then I boxed up the birds and loaded them in the back of my old square-back Honda and went for a drive.

It was a hell of a horse farm. The big iron gate at the entrance was wide open. Shiny horses of various colors grazed in green pastures, white rail fences stretching in all directions. A big fancy house sat at the end of the road. A big fancy barn to the left had a new red metal roof that extended out over a sizeable arena.

I pulled up, got out, and looked around for the owner. One of those little dogs that need clipping all the time tore out of the barn and yapped at me, dancing around like he couldn't decide whether to bite me or jump into my arms. A blond woman emerged from the same direction, wiping her hands on a rag, and walked up to me. She smelled like horses and looked like an Eddie Bauer model. "Are you here for the electrical panel?"

I said no, I was here about the baby barn swallows. She looked blank. I said, "From the wildlife clinic."

"Oh, right. Damien promised me he'd deliver them to you. My daughter was just furious that he knocked those nests down. He had to get rid of them to take the old roof off the barn. I said we could wait until they flew away, but that didn't fit his schedule." She waved at the barn in case I'd missed it. "Brittany's at school. Could you come back in about two hours? She would love to talk with you. I'm Trish, by the way."

I said no, I was here to release them and was that okay or would she be knocking down their nests again?

"Oh, no. Brittany would kill me. She loves the nests and the birds and all things great and small." She smiled and shook her head. "They teach them that stuff in school these days. Besides, the birds eat flies. You go ahead. I'll video it for her on my phone."

So we did that, and the birds did their part and took off like beautiful little rockets.

Trish was pleased. "I'm so glad they all survived."

"About half," I said, and her smile faded. "The rehab center is expensive to run. Could you make a donation to cover some of the costs?"

"Doesn't the county pay for that? I thought it was county or state or something. Like the dog pound."

"Nope. Not a dime in tax money. It's all private donations."

She considered that. "Don't people volunteer?"

"Yup. Couldn't do it without them. But there's still food and electricity and repairs. And my salary."

"Salary."

"Not much of a salary."

She fished in her pockets. "I've got ten dollars here."

And because the dog was still yapping and the barn roof was so much better than the clinic's roof and because even the standard jolt of joy when the birds flew free wasn't enough to excuse the ones that died, I said, "I was thinking more like ten thousand."

She blinked and said, "Well. No, I don't think so." She grabbed at the dog, which dodged away. I handed her a brochure and got in my car and left.

Trish showed up with Brittany about a week later. The daughter hadn't inherited her mother's cheekbones or her slenderness. She was a tough, stubby little eleven-year-old with a lot of questions about the survival rate of the birds we took in, and what did we do with the bodies of the ones that died, and did we kill the mice we fed to the birds of prey, and, if so, how did we do that?

"Can't you just feed them hawk chow or something?" her mother asked faintly.

Connie fielded most of this. Brittany kept on with the questions until she noticed that my useless new dog had stuck his nose one inch out of my office and was whipping his tail around and panting at her. He glanced at me now and then to be sure I grasped that he was being A Good Dog and staying where I'd told him. Brittany collapsed onto her knees in front of him.

"That's a pit bull," her mother said, somewhere between horror and panic.

"I think he'll be fine," I told her, not really having a clue about how the dog was with kids. But he was focused on slobbering on Brittany, until the mom pulled her away, saying, "Don't let him lick your *mouth*."

I liked the kid and had the time, so I gave the two of them a tour of the education birds. Edger Allen was a big hit, as usual. He talked crow-talk to her and took kibble from her palm with excellent manners. The mom dropped a check for fifty dollars in the collection jar on the way out, which went a fair way toward redeeming her in my eyes.

I'm easily bought, especially when the bank account is half the size of the electric bill.

I figured that was the end of it. I was busy, phoning around trying to get a new heater for the clinic donated before winter, with zero success. Baby squirrels were getting sick for no reason our vet could figure out, the state wanted its reports, and the useless white dog had to be medicated daily for a skin problem. I had a lot on my mind, which is always good since it keeps me from brooding over my personal life, such as why Kate seemed to want to be friends and nothing more. Neither part of that made any sense to me.

About a week after the Trish and Brittany invasion, Connie, the clinic's receptionist, wheeled into my office with the mail. "What's this?" she asked. Square blue envelope, hand-addressed to me. "Love note? Smells like par-fume."

It was an invitation to a party to celebrate the opening of a remodeled horse barn. I was flummoxed and then annoyed. How about a memorial service for dead swallows instead? I tossed it in the wastebasket and went back to paperwork.

The phone quit ringing for some reason and Connie got bored and came in to find out what the letter was. "None of your business," I said, not paying her much mind.

She fished it out of the wastebasket and wheeled back to her desk. Soon she was in consultation with the volunteers, principally Fred. "Hey, Sasquatch," she called after a few minutes. "You gotta clean up and go do this thing. We looked her up. Her husband's a cardiologist. This lady is rolling in it."

"I know. I've seen her place. She gave us fifty bucks and that's going to be it. I already asked her."

Connie snorted. "But she goes and invites you to this party. She's after your bod or that kid of hers has a crush on you."

Ignoring her seemed like the best strategy.

Fred cleared his throat. "Um, isn't this sort of part of your job? As executive director of the clinic? For fundraising? The heater… Just asking…" For Fred, a pale sliver of a guy, this was downright aggressive.

"You bet it is." Connie's grin was unkind. "You're stepping into the big time. Gonna need a new shirt and a haircut, buddy."

Shit. I closed the door to my office and waited for calm.

It was only a party, in a barn at that.

I hated parties, no matter the venue.

I might get to pitch people for big donations.

But I couldn't get myself to do that unless I was mad at them.

I would meet wealthy people who could put the clinic on a sound financial footing.

People who pissed me off, people who would remember for a long time if I told them how capitalism is ruining the planet.

I rubbed my face with both hands. This could not possibly go well.

At the end of the day, after the clinic was closed up, my guts were still fretting about this party. The dog and I went home and ate dinner and it became clear I wouldn't get to sleep without figuring this out.

Was this an excuse to call the ex? I'd helped a little with her move to a new house. Maybe it was only fair to ask her to help me figure this out. Not a big deal. I made the call.

"Look, Kate, I still feel bad about that kid Dylan not working out as a volunteer. How's he doing?"

"He's working at a 7-Eleven. Seems to be doing okay. Better than most of my clients. What's up?"

I winced at her assumption that I wouldn't call just to stay in touch. I told her about the party and how impossible it was.

I did not expect her to laugh.

"Sorry," she said, "this is the last thing I expected from you. I'm seeing a blind bison stumbling around in a herd of snooty gazelles," and she went off again.

"They don't even live on the same continent," I said, annoyed, and she gurgled some more.

But in the end, she said she'd help. Not for me particularly. It's what she does. She's a social worker for a reason. She said she'd come with me and that made it... possible. I hung up and went to bed with a new set of doubts.

The party was not in the remodeled barn. It was set up in the house, which was bright and airy and full of people who looked relaxed and successful. Trish, clearly a skilled hostess, steamed over to assure us that she was delighted we came. I introduced Kate as my friend. Trish put a hand on my arm to point me toward the bar table. I grabbed a beer and got Kate a glass of white wine. I turned back to find the two women chatting, Trish relaxed, Kate stiff. Trish tossed her blond head and laughed. Kate looked down and sideways the way she does when she's uncertain how to respond. Trish looked toward me, leaned close to Kate to say something, and wafted away with a big smile. Kate flushed. Blushing?

"What was that all about?" I asked.

"She thinks you're hot stuff. Amazing what a clean shirt can do for a guy. Let's go see this barn."

We wandered down a stone path toward the arena. Kate in her party clothes floated like a butterfly, one that might light on my arm if I was lucky and careful. The day was warm and bright, farmland spread around us in June sunshine.

Brittany was entertaining an audience by riding a brown horse around and around the arena. She and the horse were both totally focused on the animal's complicated footwork. We stood leaning on the rail and watched. Kate was entranced. Being that close to her, smelling her hair, stirred up a painful mix of sorrow and delight. The two months we'd been a couple had been great for me, but not for her, and I never understood why.

Hadn't she once said that social work was about second chances?

I caught hold of myself and looked around, checking for new barn swallow nests. None, but swallows dove in and out of the open arena. Horses stuck their noses out of the stalls on the far side. Brittany cantered around and around. Kate watched, smiling.

Spotting McGillvery up in the loft over the stalls canceled the peacefulness. He was pointing at the rafters and talking to a man and a woman who each held a wine glass. Lecture or sales pitch over, he scanned the crowd below. He recognized me before his eyes slid on as though he hadn't. Tell his potential customers that he treated beautiful wild animals like vermin or leave these festivities immediately? Before I made up my mind, an older lady with hair like polished silver clutched my arm. She wanted help climbing the arena fence so she could perch on the top rail rather than use the three rows of bleachers available. Not a good idea, but her mind was made up. When I had her more or less balanced, I looked around for Kate, who had vanished. I gripped the rail and scanned the arena, the path back to the house, the stalls. After a few minutes, I noticed her in the loft with McGillvery. She stood by a stack of hay bales and laughed at something he'd said.

I couldn't fault his taste. She wore a long skirt in a yellow and red pattern and a white top with no sleeves, glossy black hair loose down her back. She seems taller than she is, perfectly straight and balanced, beautiful and confident and vibrant. I turned back to Brittany in her jodhpurs and white helmet and her horse in his blue ankle wraps.

When Kate materialized again at my side, I said, "He's a son of a bitch and a liar."

"You don't get to be jealous." Smiling, but meaning it.

"Just a tip from one friend to another. Besides, another couple minutes and you'd have noticed it yourself and pushed him off the edge."

She liked that.

We wandered back inside the house. People were talking about the governor and horses and land use regulations. I was still close to bolting, with or without Kate, who seemed somehow to be having fun. McGillvery came in and moved around the room, meeting and greeting, charming people who had both money and roofs. He glanced at Kate now and then, but didn't come near us. Kate said, "He's good at schmoozing. Watch and learn. And quit looking so grumpy. You'll intimidate people."

Brittany showed up before I had to leave or publically denounce him. She called to me, "You're here! I have to shower. I'll be right back. This is my teacher." She grabbed my hand and towed me toward a woman who looked as misplaced as I felt and vanished. I figured Teacher Lori from the sixth grade and Kate and I could hang out in the Regular Folks corner until Brittany returned, then I was out of there. We agreed that we were probably here because Brittany insisted on her own guests and her parents yielded. Lori said, "Brittany is a force of nature," and kept her wine glass topped up. I downed another beer.

Lori and Kate talked about the light fixtures and the art on the walls and shelves, then Kate nudged my arm. "You're here to promote the clinic, not just stand around and glower. We talked about this, remember? Walk up to someone, say who you are and what you do. Get their name and ask about them. And *smile.* It's not that hard." She scrutinized me, then turned to Lori. "You wouldn't happen to have any bison tranquilizers on you?"

Lori looked mystified.

Kate cocked her head up at me. "That was funny. You were supposed to laugh and relax."

"Social anxiety," Lori said knowingly. "Hence, alcohol." She tipped her glass at me.

No way was I sauntering up to the local elites and making small talk. This was a mistake, and I shouldn't have pulled Kate into it. Would she come with me if I left now or would she ask Lori for a ride later? Either way, I was leaving.

But Brittany swooped in toward the three of us. "Over here. You have to stand over here." She chivied us so that our backs were to the picture window overlooking the pastures and we faced a giant wall-hung cabinet with cherry-wood doors. She darted off to a shelf and grabbed two remotes. She attacked one and curtains closed behind us, then the lights dimmed. Chatter diminished as people tried to figure out what was up.

Trish trotted over and said, "Don't start without your dad."

"I'm right here," came from a stocky guy with a hint of Brittany's intensity.

"I haven't seen this yet," Trish muttered to him. "She really, really wanted to show it at the party."

He gave her an alarmed look and held out a hand. She clutched it.

Brittany dropped one remote on the rug and worked another. The cabinet doors swung open, revealing an enormous TV screen. Kate and I raised eyebrows at each other. Guests crowded around. Kate stood close enough that I could feel her body heat.

"Okay, everyone," Brittany said, good and loud. "Stand over here so you can see the screen. This is my media project." She flashed a nervous grin at me and Lori. So that's why the teacher's here, I thought. And why am I here?

The screen brightened and held on a title slide: "Unnecessary Tragedy." Then a shot of a familiar pickup parked in front of the barn, which still had a shake roof. "McGillvery's Construction–Jobs Done Right" painted on the truck door. Doleful music. Stock photo of an adult barn swallow at a mud nest. Cut to a long video take of a sad litter of nests and baby birds struggling in the arena dust. Voice-over (Brittany):"Some people don't care. They destroy without thinking. This TRAGEDY could have been prevented just by waiting until the babies grew up."

McGillvery had knocked down a few nests, seen the havoc he was causing, and kept on doing it. Kate leaned close to my ear. "Take it easy."

The music changed to suspenseful violins. Brittany's voice intoned, "Now these babies are like refugee children, torn away from their parents." A distance shot of the cottage, zooming in slowly to the sign–Lucille Whittaker Wildlife Clinic. That I did not expect.

A still of Connie in her wheelchair behind the reception counter. "This is the place that saves birds from the people who don't care." Peppy guitar sound track. Shots of me in the office, a volunteer holding a mallard, a blurry one of the clinic cages taken through the viewing window. A shaky video of Edgar Allen Crow hopping around.

Seeing through another's eyes reminded me how dirty and depressing the clinic had been when I took over. It wasn't exactly classy now, but it was organized and tidy. The volunteers knew what they were doing. We had informational brochures and signs and outreach to local schools. We were managing fine without Trish and her friends.

The video cut to a repeat shot of nestlings in the arena dust and I winced again. Brittany's voice: "Think before you DESTROY. You can save the animals if you CARE."

Cut back to the barn, now with the new red roof, and me standing in front of my Honda. "SOME people care enough to make the world better." The music soared triumphantly as I opened one cardboard box after another and swallows zoomed out.

"Wow! You look like St. Francis blessing the animals," Kate whispered.

THE END in fancy script.

I stood with my mouth open while Kate led the applause, teacher Lori and the parents close behind. The rest of the guests, after a stunned pause, joined in. I pulled myself together and looked around for McGillvery, who wasn't anywhere in sight.

Brittany wasn't done. She squared her shoulders and faced her audience. "Mom and I saw the clinic, and it's a rotten old house. Everyone should give them some money to fix it up so it's better for the birds. Right, Mom?"

Brittany turned to look at her mother with battle in her eyes.

Trish took a breath. "You are absolutely right, dear, and we have the clinic manager here tonight. I'm sure he'd be glad to answer any questions."

Brittany's lips tightened. Before her daughter could speak, Trish said, "And, uh, I'll be forming a committee to help their board with fundraising strategies." An aside to me—"You do have a board?"

"Yes. Yes, we do." A board of three ancients, all named Whittaker, who had a hard time remembering who I was. No need to go into that.

Brittany beamed—a happy little girl—and if she showed a flash of triumph for an instant, it was only because I was looking for it.

An hour or so later, we thanked Trish and Brittany, and I drove us through the big iron gate and along the winding road in the twilight. After a peaceful silence, Kate said, "Every time I'm with you it's an adventure or a disaster or a surprise. You hit a triple tonight."

"Sorry you came?"

"Oh, no." A little laugh-snort. "The blind bison falls into the money pit. No, that doesn't work. I drank too much of that excellent wine. I've never seen you like that. Eloquent, almost." Then, dreamily, "And I've never seen your cabin in decent weather. It must be nice."

I said it was and she could see for herself tonight.

She was asleep in another half mile.

I drove the country road through moonlight, wondering what the price was for this much happiness and trying to decide whether I might have paid in advance.

# Toxins

The symbol of our great nation looked like a drunk in the gutter. Grubby white head and tail, ominous yellow beak, disheveled brown feathers. The eagle was sprawled across the bottom of a ditch, wings spread toward either bank, feet in a trickle of agricultural runoff, baleful yellow eyes daring me to mess with it. The day was hot and bright and my shirt stuck to my back. Up the bank, cars hissed on the highway. If the occupants saw me, they must have wondered what a guy wearing welders' gloves was doing staggering around in the weeds and the mud.

The eagle floundered down the gully with me lunging after it, hoping to grab both its legs at the same time, the better to avoid powerful talons locking onto any of my body parts. Slipped to my knees, mud and muck everywhere, and, eventually, success. Except for that big eagle beak way too near my face. I lurched to my feet, a leg in each hand, the wings more or less confined between my body and an elbow, but without a third hand to grab the head.

Coming alone on this call was dumb as a hemlock stump, especially given that I had little experience with eagles. But I hadn't really believed it was an eagle. I'd gone after swans that were Canada geese, a peregrine falcon that turned out to be a parrot, and a possum mistaken for a baby cougar. This was meant to be a red-tailed hawk, a considerably more manageable bird.

Poison, broken wing, or collision with electric wires might account for the eagle's sorry state. This was not the time to figure it out. I staggered up the bank, slipping and panting, to my old Honda, eager to stuff this bird into the big dog carrier in the rear before it got itself organized to bite a chunk out of me. The car was unlocked but the rear hatch was, of course, shut.

I stood soaked in sweat and cursing, trying to figure out how to grab both legs in one glove to free a hand to open up the hatch. Cars slowed but didn't stop. The sun didn't let up. I was six kinds of moron, overheated ones.

The eagle's head began trembling, and it opened its beak to gasp a couple of times. The rest of the big bird went limp.

Turned out I could hold both legs in one hand. Got the hatch open, stuffed the bird in the carrier, and headed for the vet.

An anxious fifteen miles later, Dr. Hanson took charge of the eagle and said she'd let me know what she found. Nothing more I could do, so I drove to my cabin with the Honda's air conditioner roaring, intent on a cool shower.

Back at the rehab center in fresh jeans and shirt, I was unsettled from sun and adrenaline. The volunteers had let the dog out of my office and he slunk back in guiltily and curled up on his bed. Connie abandoned her reception duties long enough to bring me up to speed–several intakes, mostly not-yet-competent fledgling song birds; a hundred phone queries; a window-strike kestrel that died. The volunteers had not found or created any fresh disasters. Briefing over, she spun her wheelchair back to her desk, and I settled in to eat a sandwich and research the government paperwork that eagles require.

Brooding about the eagle was a welcome change from mourning Kate's too-brief return to my life. The night after Trish Kogan's party had been terrific from my perspective and she'd suggested a sequel the next morning even though it made her late to work. But that was a week ago and I hadn't heard from her since. She hadn't returned my calls or emails. I yanked out a drawer and pawed through files looking for the eagle folder.

Before I got very far, Trish Krogan herself swooped into my office without warning and nailed me with her neat red talons. Metaphorically. Brittany, her intense eleven-year-old daughter, had veered off to inspect the turtle tank on Connie's desk.

"Do you have a minute?" Trish asked, sitting herself down in the guest chair. She settled in with a graceful certainty born of good looks and money. The ugly dog wagged his tail and got up from his bed to sniff her thigh. She eyed him with suspicion and failed to pet. She said, "Isn't this weather something? I'm so glad it wasn't so hot at the party." A quick smile and small talk was over. "We need to make a plan, and I've got some time right now. You remember our conversation at the party?"

I did, but hadn't really believed she would tackle the slowly decaying organization that is the Lucille Whittaker Wildlife Center, even to please her passionate animal-loving daughter. I nodded and went back to my sandwich. "This is my first chance to eat." The dog gave up on her and settled his butt where he could stare at me, shifting his forefeet now and then to remind me he was there.

Trish crossed her arms over her shirt. "I've done arts and school campaigns, but not this sort of project before. I talked to some friends with experience. They suggest that first we should go for a capital project and then an endowment to cover some of operations. Immediate needs, then long term stability. Sound right?"

"Sounds great." I tossed a crust to the dog and tidied papers on my desk, buying time. The dog gulped the inappropriate people-food and curled back up. "You've got some ideas for raising money? I'm all ears."

Brittany's voice carried into my office. "I *know* the ones with red on their heads aren't native. What are you doing to save the *real* western painted turtles?"

Connie's answer was lower pitched and I didn't try to follow it.

Trish's goal had to be bonding with her daughter over animal welfare and the environment and global healing.

She said, "Oh, yes. I'm drafting a strategy. I met with your board, and I think we can work with them."

"You've already talked to my board?" I didn't mean to sound horrified.

"I know it's delicate. They really don't have any energy, but they feel a sense of ownership. We'll set up an advisory committee with some experienced people and keep them in the loop."

"You *met* with them?"

Trish shifted in her seat. "Well, an opportunity came up unexpectedly. My mother-in-law knows Alma and George Whittaker. They all live in the same retirement center. They play bridge. I probably should have checked with you first, but there they were in the dining hall, and Wilson Whittaker was visiting, so it was your whole board, and we all had dinner at the same table. The food is not bad there, not bad at all. I was discreet, really. I just made inquiries."

Right. Just made inquiries. I took a breath.

The board and I met at the Cascadia Café in town for coffee three times a year. The surviving Whittakers would tell me about Lucille and how much she had loved birds and her summer cabin in the woods where I now lived. I would tell them a few stories about animals we'd succeeded in releasing. The Whittakers wrote the same checks every December to semi-fund the center and did a fine job of staying out of my way.

Trish gave me another moment to catch up, but it was bound to be a short one.

Brittany bounded in without her usual air of serious evaluation. "Edgar is out there! He's up on a perch! He was so quiet I didn't see him." She whirled to me. "I need kibble to feed him." She got hold of herself. "Please." Then, "Why is he loose? What's he doing in the reception area?"

I explained that he was camping in the reception area because the night heron had his cage. Dr. Hanson said the wing bone was healed, and the heron needed to regain muscle strength so we could release him. We didn't have a proper flight cage. The crow cage would have to do. I'd spent half a day setting up a stock tank with rocks and water and gold fish and changing the perches. I gave Brittany some kibble and she quick-stepped back out to the reception area to commune with the crow.

I sat up straighter and made eye contact with Trish. It would be hopelessly dumb not to take advantage of her energy and fundraising experience. Channeling it, that was what was needed. "A capital campaign sounds good. We really need a new roof and a new heater. Winter's coming."

Trish shook her head. "You need a new *building*. The Whittakers agreed that it was a miracle this place hasn't fallen down yet. I don't think they'll object."

"That would be great, but we have to get through the winter first."

"Of course. I'll see if Damien McGillvery will patch the roof for free–he needs the positive PR and I'll see it gets noticed by his customer base–and we'll find some kind of heater."

Damien McGillvery? The contractor who dumped baby barn swallows on the ground to die? Suck up to that asshole to get the roof fixed? I opened my mouth and shut it again.

Trish hesitated, then rolled on about events and major donors and grants. I nodded and said "uh-huh" until she finished up. "Well, those are my preliminary ideas. I'll send you an email with a draft of the strategy, and you can think it over. Oh, and if you get any special animals in, endangered or cute or something, let me know. We can use that for publicity."

"We'll likely get a bald eagle in a few days. It's at the vet now."

"That would be perfect. Great for a kick-off event or at least some photos we can use later. Let me know."

I pulled up my executive director socks even higher. "This sounds really good, Trish. We can use the help."

Brittany came in and sat on the floor to pet the dog. Trish eyed this uneasily. "Don't let him lick you. Give him some space or he might bite."

Brittany, the dog, and I all ignored this.

"Edgar won't eat any more kibble," Brittany said. "What if he gets out?"

"He won't," I told her. "And if he does, he comes back. This is his home."

Trish leaned forward. "I need to ask whether you are totally up for this campaign." She looked at Brittany. The dog was on his back, legs in the air, having his belly scratched. "Honey, why don't you go outside? See if you can find some interesting bugs or something."

Alarm bells rang in the back of my head, but real executive directors do not evade development tidal waves. I told Brittany, "You can take the dog out. He probably needs to pee."

"We're going to the creek," she told her mother. "Connie says a turtle lives there."

"Stay safe. Don't go in the water."

When we were alone, Trish said, "I can't raise real money without your full engagement. That could mean some changes."

I reared back. "Full engagement? I always make fundraising a priority, but I have to run this place, and there's only so many hours in the day."

She tilted her head. "That's not quite what I mean. How to say this? You're in kind of a backwater here, and there's not a lot of... pressure. You do your own thing your own way and that's fine. But I'll need you to be out front and talking to people, presenting a vision, for this to happen."

I was pretty sure I wasn't getting what she meant.

She nodded and smiled. "I've seen you do it, at the party at my house. It's just more a matter of… appearances. Style."

I'd raised a month's budget pitching the care center at her party, but that was a fluke and we both knew it. "You're talking about, what, better clothes and making speeches? Charming people." Way more than putting up with McGillvery.

She beamed at me. "Exactly! Expanding your skill set just a little. I can help and so can your girlfriend. Kate? I think that's her name. She's very nice."

"She's not my girlfriend."

"Friend, then. I have to go. I'll send you that email. I think we can work together, really. It will be fun."

We shook hands, she retrieved her daughter and departed. I sat without moving until the dog nudged me to see if his kibble and crust source was still alive.

The next day, Dr. Hanson reported that the eagle's coordination was a little better. The test results weren't back, but she was treating it for lead poisoning anyway. "Classic presentation," she said. Eagles used to get poisoned by eating wounded ducks full of shot, but waterfowl hunters switched to non-lead ammo years ago. People shoot at eagles now and then, but she said the x-ray didn't show any bullets, just a few suspicious-looking spots. We speculated that the bird probably picked up lead fragments from a deer carcass.

Dr. Hanson was as engaged as I was at this chance to help a charismatic bird–a top predator, national icon, and one big raptor. We kicked around how to pay for salmon as the bird recovered and started eating. My bigger worry was that the clinic didn't have a good space for a bird that size. We could handle it until it picked up strength–and I got Trish her publicity shots–then I'd need to find another facility.

Dr. Hanson wanted to keep the eagle a few more days before we took it for follow-up care. Fine with me. I had plenty to deal with already at the clinic.

Trish sent me a three page email, which I was too busy to read.

A couple days later, I was at the cabin microwaving frozen lasagna for dinner, door open because of the heat, the dog crashed out in the middle of the floor, when Kate called.

"Hey," she said, "I'm really sorry I haven't been in touch. My case load is up by half and it's been crazy." Her voice was a touch too cheerful and relaxed and carefully heedless of the questions vibrating between us. Or maybe just in me.

She said, "Anyway, I hear Trish Krogan is going to transform the rehab center into a marvel of modern veterinary medicine."

"And how did you happen to hear that?"

"I ran into her at the cafe where I get lunch. It's a small town."

"One of Trish Krogan's super-powers is running into the people in my life. What'd she say?"

"Let's you and me do lunch. I'll tell you everything."

No response for almost two weeks and now I was supposed to drop everything? "You know I don't 'do lunch'. I've got a clinic to run. It's the busy season."

"Tomorrow's the only day I have lunch hour free for weeks. Please? You know the café. I'll be there at quarter to noon. You can buy."

I found out it wasn't in me to say no and stick to it.

For sure I was a fool.

I ate lasagna with the dog waiting patiently for me to put the dish on the floor. A book about wolves kept my brain distracted for the rest of the evening.

I showed up at the cafe a minute or two late with a small smear of bird poop on a shirt that had been clean until a volunteer needed a hand.

Kate was studying the menu at a table in a back corner. She looked great, as usual, even in her subdued social worker clothes. When she looked up and met my eye, the usual jolt went through me. "Well," I said, "you whistled and the bison came."

She smiled and handed over a menu as I sat down. "Don't sulk. Trish wants me to help with this fundraising campaign for the clinic."

"Anything for you."

"She's all about image. That button-up shirt is a start, but no plaid, please. Something in blue would look good on you. Score some jeans or khakis without stains and footwear that isn't boots, and we'll call it good."

I sat for a moment and then forced a smile. "Trish gave you the buff and fluff assignment. If she wants me to shave, the whole thing is off."

"She probably does. Just take the hedge clippers to it a little."

After we'd ordered, she tilted her head at me and her voice changed from chipper to persuasive. "I think Trish is worth the trouble. She can do a lot for the clinic. I get that she's pretty high-powered and it's a new level of fundraising, but I've seen you do this. You might even like being sociable with people who appreciate what you do."

First a makeover and now a pep talk. A conspiracy to improve me.

Clarification of why we weren't a couple.

"If you want, I could help you with your pitch, maybe after work someday. Practice for wooing the local one percent."

I leaned back in my chair, away from her. "So now you're Trish's assistant."

She said, "Don't be grumpy. I couldn't possibly want to see you because I like you or because you'll have a good story from the clinic. But, yes, she thought I could help and I'd like to."

That took some of the edge off. While we waited for the food, I told her about the eagle and not just to head off more ideas from Trish. Talking with Kate had always come easy. "Handling a bird that powerful–well, it's awesome. The test results came in and it's got lead poisoning. Leaks into the nervous system and the bird just runs down and can't do anything. One more victim of the toxins we turn loose in the environment."

"People get lead poisoning, too. Especially kids, from old paint chips and paint dust. Very hard on them cognitively."

I nodded. She's in charge of the people problems.

We ate and I remembered to ask about her work. She talked about angry teenagers and lousy parents, about the crimes they commit against the world and each other, and somehow managed to put a positive twist on all of that.

Restaurants make me uncomfortable, especially crowded ones. Noisy and claustrophobic. That, and the echoes of the plan to renovate me.

We finished eating and Kate said, "Trish wants to start with local appearances to–she actually said 'build the brand'–before the big campaign. Don't you love the lingo? She'd like to set up a talk at the senior center where the Whittakers live. Can you do that? Maybe bring one of the animals? It sounds like an easy way to start the campaign."

The waiter dropped off the check and I dug out my wallet. "I give a talk there every year before Thanksgiving with the raven or the owl. The Whittakers ask me to, mostly to entertain their friends. The residents never donate much."

Kate nodded encouragingly, maybe the way she nodded to a kid who'd pulled his grades up.

"I apply to a half dozen or so foundations every year, which takes a ton of time. A couple of them haven't turned us down yet."

She blinked, surprised.

Might as well run up the score–"The email solicitations do OK–the Christmas one better than the spring one. And of course I'm always begging for in-kind donations, like pet food and printing our brochure."

Kate tilted her head. "I didn't know you do all that."

Yeah, not a complete wash-out. "Always more to do than I have the time for."

"Maybe Trish can help with that."

Maybe Trish was all about great ideas for what *I* could do.

We stood up to go. I held the door for her and hesitated outside.

"See?" Kate said. "Lunch in a cafe isn't so bad." The wind blew her black hair across her face and she brushed it away, smiling. "Next time we'll do it your way and eat granola bars on a cliff somewhere. Hang in there with Trish. I checked her out and she's a powerhouse. It won't kill you to dude up a bit and smile more." She stood on tip-toe to give me a kiss on my cheek. "It's good to see you."

I watched her walk toward her office with an acid mix of regret, frustration, and feelings too murky to name. Whatever had gone wrong between wasn't going to get fixed. Given enough time and distance, the ache would go away. Eventually.

Trish called me two days later to set up a photo shoot with the eagle. "The vet called me this morning," I told her. "The eagle died last night." The bird had not rallied much and nothing Dr. Hanson tried had helped. She was a good vet and felt as bad about it as I did. Which was pretty bad. Despite its battered state, it had been a beautiful bird and it died because humans didn't want to change out lead shot for something less toxic.

"Darn," Trish said, "That's too bad. What else could we use? The photographer is a friend and he's only in town for a couple of days."

I breathed in and out for a bit, then said, "I suppose we could use the night heron. It's about ready for release."

"Is it big? Is it pretty?"

"It would do."

"I'm seeing this as business casual, not a sports coat, but not too woodsy, you know what I mean? Professional. Has Kate talked to you?"

"Kate talked to me." I'd been replaying that lunch conversation ever since.

I told her we could not disrupt the bird for photography–we could lose our permit for that. We set up the shoot for the next morning and gathered at the outdoor cage. I positioned a lanky guy with an SLR cannon well back, opened the cage door, and put in the mice and fish carcasses. He got a couple of shots before the bird starting thinking about making a break for it and I had to close the door. The photographer wasn't very satisfied.

Trish told me she was thinking about a script and finding a videographer for a promo piece, but her top priority was getting an architect on board to design the new building. "Then we can cost it out. I've got a few friends who might make significant donations to kick off the building fund. I'm still revising the publicity plan I sent you. More pieces keep cropping up."

This new building would be floating somewhere in fantasy land for a long time, possibly forever. I said, "We still need a roof and heater to get through the winter." If taking a favor from that bird-murdering McGillvery was the price, I would pay it.

"Like I said, that won't be a problem." And she took off with her friend to show him an old corral he was just going to love to photograph, moss all over it. Connie watched them go, sucked on her lower lip, and didn't say a word.

I went back to answering emails until I needed to show a new volunteer how to feed baby raccoons. The phone never stopped. Connie's voice was a constant background sound.

That evening, the volunteers finally left, and it was my time to settle, a couple of hours alone for record keeping, for leaving phone messages in reply to phone messages, for checking on a pair of flickers that weren't doing well. Trish was a burr in my sock, catching my attention when I didn't expect it, warning me that the future looked complicated.

A car pulled into the parking lot and I sagged. One more person's animal problem. But it was Kate.

She sauntered in as though it wasn't the first time she had set foot in the clinic for months. She was still wearing office clothes–a gray skirt and red blouse with a faint pattern.

"Hey," I said. "Late in the day for a visit."

"I told you I'd drop by. This is the only time I can ever catch you, when everyone else is home for dinner. Guapo, how's my buddy?" She'd named the dog "handsome" in Spanish when she met him that night after Trish's party. He wagged and clawed at her skirt with enthusiasm. She scratched his spine and he nearly melted. "I heard about the eagle. I'm so sorry."

Heard about it from Trish, unless she had a brand-new connection to Dr. Hanson.

Kate appropriated one of the granola bars I keep on a shelf and ate it while she fussed with the dog. I finished an email, shut down the computer, and made my final rounds. She hadn't said what she was doing here and I didn't ask.

I locked up and we stood on the front porch listening to barred owls talking, maybe parents and kids. "Whoo cooks for *you*." The day had slid into dusk, but it was still warm. Traffic pounded by on the road. I couldn't hear the creek–too dry, too low. I waited, balanced on a precipice I didn't yet have words for.

Kate said, "Trish is worried you might not be okay working with that roofer–McGillvery? He has to be on site now and then to do the job. I think she's afraid you'll punch him out." Smiling, but serious.

The owls kept talking and the cars kept moving homeward. The dog snuffled around the dump box. I felt soaked in fatigue.

"Hey?" she said. "You okay with this?"

I looked at her for a long moment, taking her in, storing it away.

"Kate. I will warp myself, up to a point, to work with Trish. And McGillvery. This is the job I've chosen and I'll do it the best I can. The clinic needs what they have to offer. What I hope they have to offer." I took a deep breath and smelled dust. "But I can't be your project."

The smile faltered and she drew back. "What? 'My project'?" She shook her head and stared at me. "That's not what this is. I want what Trish is doing to succeed. I'm trying to be on the team." Surprised and hurt. "We're *friends*."

I looked out at the trees, listless from the drought, some of the maples yellowing early. "We can't be friends. Not like this."

Her black brows drew together, not understanding.

I said, "You can't be part of this. That, I cannot do. It's too hard."

The security light flickered, trying to decide whether it was dark enough yet to come on.

I said, mostly to myself, "It looks like we really are done."

Her face changed. Crumpled. She started to say something and stopped.

I hesitated between unbearables. Then I brushed a hand down her hair in passing, let the dog into the backseat of the car, and drove on out of the parking lot, not at all sure I could merge into traffic without crashing.

# The Night Heron on the Way to Bellingham

The city park was hot, the late afternoon air thick and dusty. I hoped for a breeze off the lake, but no such luck. The night heron stamped and rustled in the big dog crate at my feet. I'd picked this park for a release site because I knew night herons roosted here. The vet said the broken bone was good, but no way to be certain about the muscles. The bird had flapped from perch to perch in the crow enclosure, but the cage wasn't long enough for real flight. I'd notified the woman who found the bird about the release, but she didn't want any part of it.

I sat on a bench near the edge of the lake and waited, sat and groused to myself about having to tear off to Bellingham, Washington, nearly 400 miles north, as soon as this was over. The last place on earth I wanted to go.

Super-volunteer Janie would close up today and take care of the dog. I'd be available by phone. It would be okay. Maybe.

Why Missy thought this trip was necessary escaped me.

I would turn the heron loose and hit the road. Drive until I was drowsy, pull over and sleep, get into Bellingham tomorrow morning. Missy wouldn't want me showing up after midnight and waking her kids. I had a backpack with a change of clothes and a toothbrush. Couldn't think of anything else I'd need, except a lot more tolerance than I had in stock.

Years ago, it had been a big deal to get out of the town where I was raised. I'd made it only a state and a half south, close enough to be reeled back in. Family was in short supply. Missy was pretty much it and I'd said I would come.

A couple dozen crows winged across the dimming sky, silent, heading for their night roost. They bunch up this time of year, late summer, when the fledglings can fly. Parents and kids, aunts and uncles, cousins and grandparents all wanting to be together.

Waiting with the heron, waiting for show-time, I dredged up the names of my stepfather's two brothers and their wives. Didn't succeed with most of their kids. Step-cousins. Was that a real category? No basis for a real relationship, that I did know.

First I had to get through this release and that was going to be complicated. Everything Trish touched got complicated. Connie was supposed to be part of this, if she could get away from the clinic's reception desk in time. I should have encouraged her to come on releases more often, the best part of wildlife rehabilitation. She'd reacted to this one the way I expected: "Trish wants a stage prop, right? Me in the wheelchair–diversity and all that horse shit–to suck up to the robber barons." I backed off and said to give this a pass if she wanted–I'd include her in the next release. But she was curious enough and bored enough to say she'd try to come. Or maybe just doing me a favor.

A middle-aged couple in identical beige shorts and running shoes walked by on the bark-chip path that ran around the lake. Their beagle strained at his leash, eager to make the acquaintance of the heron. I was about to tell them to keep it away, when I saw Kate in the distance walking toward me. Quick as a leg cramp, my stomach knotted.

A little bit of brains kicked in. We were sure to run into each other now and then. People walk in the park, all sorts of people, at all hours. Could be just a coincidence. Right.

She was zeroed in on me. Her mouth was tight and her shoulders tense. Even the black hair didn't have its usual swing. She looked stressed out.

Her problems weren't my problems. I couldn't afford to care.

The couple dragged their dog off and continued on their way around the lake.

Kate arrived and planted herself in front of me, slim and vivid in a skirt with yellow flowers swirling.

"What brings you here?" I asked.

"I need to talk to you."

"This isn't the best time." Talk about what? I was done coming when she whistled. "How'd you know I was here?"

"Janie told me. You weren't at the clinic." Her hands were in fists, chin stuck out. "I know it's over between us, but I still need to clear the air. To apologize. I have not been my best self with you. Not even close. I shouldn't have—"

"This is the bird? It's in there?"

We both flinched. An older guy lugging a video camera with a TV station logo.

I stood up and swiveled between him and Kate. "Yeah. This is the bird."

Kate looked derailed, mouth still open.

He put the camera down. "The light won't hold for long. Where you going to turn it loose? Will it fly or just walk away?" He frowned at Kate. "You must be the woman?"

I shook my head at him and turned to Kate. "Trish set this up. He's going to shoot the release and they'll air it on the news as human interest or something. Publicity. Part of the new building campaign."

Kate didn't look any less fuddled.

Connie rolling up didn't help. She was still in the lavender scrubs she wore at the clinic. The harsh light made her look tired. Tired and older. One wheel moved off the asphalt and bogged down on the bark path. She wrestled it back before I dared try to help.

"Oh, you're the one they said," the camera man said. "Let's make this happen. I can get all three of you in the shot if you two move over on the right and you stand in front with the crate—"

"What's she here for?" Connie demanded.

"Damned if I know anymore," Kate said. "I didn't expect the circus."

Connie spun her wheelchair closer. "You watch your mouth, young woman. You've got a fat nerve, showing up to grab the glory after the way you behave."

Kate straightened up, shaking her head. "What glory? I didn't know anything about this."

"So why are you here?"

Kate took a step back. "I don't think that's any of your business. What do you mean about the way I behave?"

"Oh, it's my business all right." Connie's glare was molten.

I had no idea what she was talking about. For about another thirty seconds.

"Listen, young woman. You don't know the gloom coming out of that office every time you show up and then flit off. There's a word for girls like you and it's not a nice one. I know what's going on—I pay way more attention than anyone thinks. You just step in and out as you like and leave a good man cut to ribbons. There's names for you, all right."

"Whoa! Connie—stand down," I said, but she didn't hear a word.

"You don't know the first thing about it!" Kate said. "Who are you to judge anyone?"

The camera man said, "Ladies, we need to shoot this before it gets dark."

"I'm the one watching this stupid on-again/off again dance, that's who."

Kate had her own glare turned on. "You have *no idea* what it's like to be with him–he never says a word about what he's thinking. You have to *guess*. It's not like being with a normal person who wants to grab a beer or go to a concert or do anything fun. And that cabin is *dire* in winter. Things *freeze* in there. So don't you go telling me I haven't tried. Because I have."

A snort and a sneer. "Not nearly hard enough. You want parties? You are a fool, and your foolishness is nothing but trouble. You need to fish, cut bait, or get the hell out of the boat."

"You are no one to be telling me what to do!"

"Somebody sure needs to. You're a damn wrecking ball is what you are."

"Ladies? The light is going. Could this wait?"

The couple with the beagle had circled back.

"Hey," I said, "Could you keep the dog away? There's a bird in there and he's scaring it." The women were scaring me.

"Is this one of those flash mobs?" the man asked. "I've seen those on YouTube. Is this like a play or something?"

"No way, Jimmy," the woman said. "It's gotta be an indie film. Maybe it's a student project from that film school in Eugene."

Kate said, "You know what he's like! He says 'sure' to everything and you never know if he's going to do it or not."

"And that's such a big damn deal to you? You keep looking for perfection and you're gonna die alone, girl. Trust me on this one."

"'Scuse me, folks. Everything OK here?" Park security, a large guy sweating in a black uniform, frowning at us all.

"We don't need any cop," said Connie.

"Keep that damn dog away," I said and realized I might be just a little frazzled.

"Bad language makes for weak dialog," said the beagle man. "David Mamet excepted."

"We are having a discussion," Kate said. "And I was just leaving."

"Sounds more like an argument," the guard said, which was reasonable enough. "You all could maybe keep it down some."

"No problem," I said.

"I seen you somewhere before," the guard said to the camera man.

"I'm from KACD, channel 11. I do weather so that's probably where you saw me. Ten o'clock. Nine years on the air. I do video, too."

"Really. What's happening here?" The guard seemed to have all the time in the world.

"It's a drama," said the beagle man. "Some kind of production. It's not a commercial–no product and anyway commercials always have lots of lights and wires. This one's on the cheap."

"Cheap? I don't think so, "said the camera man. "I'm filming a human interest spot with some bird. I thought it was *Animal Planet*, but it's looking more like *Judge Judy* meets *The Bachelor*."

"Cute," the beagle woman said. "Let's stay and watch."

"I could watch *her* all day," said her companion. He was looking at Kate.

"Keep that dog back," I said.

"Move over that way," said the camera man, pointing.

"He's easy on the eyes, too," the woman said. They dragged their dog back a few feet, toenails scrabbling in protest. The guard crossed his arms and stepped out of the way. Kate moved aside, but she didn't leave. The camera guy made me drag the carrier into better light and put Connie on one side and me on the other.

When he said he was ready, I took a breath and tried to look calm and competent instead of seriously rattled. I opened the carrier door and a whole lot of nothing happened. We waited, me standing alongside the carrier, Connie camped on the other side. The camera man, kneeling in front and to one side with the camera on his shoulder, started looking impatient. Probably his knees hurt.

"Isn't something supposed to happen?" beagle man asked. His dog whined.

We all glared at him and he shut up. The dog didn't.

I was starting to think I'd have to grab the bird and pull it out, which I did not want to do. I made "wait" motions with my hands. After too many minutes, a sturdy dark beak poked out, with two suspicious red eyes. The bird studied this unexpected chance at a jail break. Abruptly, in a blur of black and white, it floundered out and stood hunched for a second, then it opened its wings and flapped mightily, the yellow legs trailing behind. It flew low and awkwardly to a bush growing in the lake and crash-landed on a too-thin branch.

The kind of release you dread. The bird isn't up to normal strength, but flies well enough that it's impossible to recapture. Damn.

"Perfect!" said the camera man.

"Wow!" said the guard.

"Cool!" said the beagle lady. "That was great."

The dog yelped and scrabbled against the leash, trying desperately to go for the bird.

Connie and I didn't say anything. Neither did Kate.

"Well, that's my bit," said the camera man. "This will get edited into the interview you did yesterday. The lighting was not bad, not bad at all." He nodded to me and Kate and stepped carefully around Connie. "Good luck sorting out your issues."

The couple and their dog meandered on down the path. The guard asked what kind of bird it was. I told him and he ambled off.

Connie and I shrugged at each other. "Well, I'll see you in a few days," she said. I knew better than to offer her to help her get into her van. She had a system and didn't appreciate any hint that she couldn't manage on her own. She gave Kate a final glare and rolled off, the wheelchair bumping on the rough path, then across the lawn and onto the sidewalk.

It became quiet. The sun was easing itself down somewhere behind us.

The heron shuffled around on top of the bush.

After a minute, Kate asked, "Will it be okay? It didn't seem to fly very well."

I wagged my hand "maybe." "It can catch enough frogs and goldfish in the shallows to survive until it builds up muscle." I tried to sound confident.

And I guess I did, because Kate said, "It gets a another chance. What your work is all about."

What she did, too, helping kids entangled in the criminal justice system. I hadn't thought of that, of us in different versions of the same sort of business.

Time to take the carrier and leave, but instead I found myself sitting on the bench.

She sat down, too, and didn't say anything for a space. Then, "I shouldn't have bought into Trish's agenda to change you, to turn you into a slick salesman for the clinic. That's what I came to say. It was disrespectful."

I wasn't sure that was the right word, but it would do. "Apology accepted." Now she would leave.

Kate said, "Connie loves you. She really lit into me."

"She makes stuff up." I stood up.

"I don't think so. Can we just sit here for a while?"

Where was this going? "Why?" I sat back down.

She used both hands to push her hair back. "It's a nice evening to sit in the park." She stuck her sandals out and examined her toes. "Janie said you were going to Bellingham. She didn't know why, but she said it seemed to be a big deal."

Across the lake, mallards quacked and flapped around in the water. I thought about it, the space she'd left open for me to use or ignore. Hell, what harm could it do? "My stepfather is dying, some kind of heart failure. My sister wants me to go see him. Talk and hug and forgive him. That sort of thing. It's important to her."

Kate was quiet for a minute. Then, "You never talk about your family. I didn't know you have a sister. And a stepfather who needs forgiving."

"I wouldn't say he needs it. Doesn't much deserve it, either."

A jogger loped by, a chubby guy puffing hard. Doctor probably told him he'd get diabetes if he didn't exercise.

We sat on the bench in the dusk not touching. A cat yowled in the distance. A streetlight behind us came on.

"Maybe you could tell me about him?" Her voice was hesitant, as if she were asking a favor.

"You won't like me any better." Harsher than I meant.

"Can we just talk for just for a few minutes? Isn't that okay?"

Something was wrong with her voice. I knew the vigor and confidence she projected weren't always real, but she'd never let them lapse like this before. Maybe she was in some kind of predicament and working up to ask for my help. Hit the road or sit with her? I made the usual decision. "All right, but I have to go soon."

Stick with the short version. "My mom married Roger–my stepfather–when I was about six and they had the two girls, Missy and Mandy. We were a family for a while, in Bellingham. She died when I was thirteen and I moved out after high school. Was thrown out. Got in a couple years of college. Tried a bunch of different jobs. I drifted down here, stumbled on the rehab center, and volunteered. I took the job when the director moved on." I'd discovered that wildlife made the world more tolerable and found a way to fix a little of the destruction people did.

"You and Roger didn't get along?"

She was good at listening. It was easier to go with it than walk away.

"I was bigger than him by the time I was fifteen and I kept on going. Then when I was a freshman in high school, I was in a scuffle, not even a real fight. But I broke out a kid's front teeth, so I was on a watch-list forever after at high school. Roger ragged on me about fighting, which I never did, and obeying every rule he could come up with, which I didn't do either. He lectured me a lot about respecting women and giving the girls privacy."

She got it. "He thought you were a risk to his daughters."

"The girls didn't understand–hell, at the time *I* didn't get what he was so worried about–but they were developing and Roger freaked. Who knows? Maybe I *was* a threat. He kicked me out the week I graduated from high school. Cold turkey. I should have seen it coming, but I didn't." That shock–being despised for who I was, not for anything I'd done. Finding out that "family" was revocable.

"I see this a lot with teenagers. At least he waited until you graduated."

I couldn't see that the timing much mattered. "I was on my own." A memory of family: all of us at the dinner table, then me tearing around the house with Missy on my shoulders, Mom laughing. Mandy jealous, wanting a turn even though she thought this was kid stuff. Was Roger uneasy even then? Was I inventing a happiness that never really existed? Maybe the memory was vivid because happy times were rare.

Kate shattered that train of thought. "Look!" Pointing. The heron had leapt off the bush and was flying low over the lake, working hard. Could night herons swim? I wasn't sure. It was close to landing in the drink and, for all I knew, drowning itself. But it kept on, just above the water, and disappeared on the other side. I said, "Definitely flying better." We sat back with little sighs of relief.

"How did your mom die?" The uncertainty was gone. She had her footing again, safe in the neighborhood of her profession.

"She got cancer. Roger did his best for her. He did love her."

"And you did, too. What was she like?"

"Why do you want to know?"

"Because you usually won't talk about anything important."

"This is important?"

She sighed. "Yessssss."

"Mom and I got along fine. Great, even, and it was okay with Roger and the little girls. I guess she was the glue."

"Was your biological dad in the picture?"

"No. She got pregnant by some guy–she wouldn't tell me his name or anything else–and dropped out of college and had me." I rolled my shoulders forward to shrug it off. "Roger handed me twenty dollars and said the hardware store was hiring. That was it. Didn't even want me for Thanksgiving. Missy and I stay in touch." I straightened on the bench. "I should have hung in with that kid you sent me. Dylan."

"Dylan's fine. Not every placement works out. Missy is your only family, then."

"Pretty much. Mandy doesn't like me anymore than her father does."

I smelled a cigarette before I saw a guy walking by, the tip glowing red. He looked toward us and went on his way.

Kate said, "I really hate it that you thought I was treating you like a project. Fixing you."

I didn't say anything.

"It *was* a project–sort of–but not like that."

"What *were* you doing?" Besides confirming I wouldn't do as-is. And why the hell was she sticking around?

She was looking at the heron or maybe the mallards. "I was trying to figure out if there was another way to be with you. So I tried working with you and Trish on fundraising for the clinic. It seemed like a reasonable idea at the time."

Past time to put an end to this. "We tried and it didn't work. I'm not the kind of person you're looking for." The familiar ache was back. Time to get on the road and face a different set of troubles.

She spoke so softly I could barely hear. "So why can't I just walk away?" Her shoulder twitched. She said, a little louder, "You seemed so isolated and shut down. Those weeks we were together? I felt like you were buried in a thick down jacket, all muffled up. I could never get through the jacket. It was lonely."

I couldn't help myself. "Maybe not the jacket, but you got the rest off."

Her teeth flashed white in the dimness as she grinned. "Yes, I did manage that. And I have to say, it was worth the trouble."

"Indeed it was." That first time, both of us desperate to get down to skin, both of us wary, until we weren't...

"I remember telling you I wasn't made of glass, that you weren't going to break me."

"I try to be careful."

She leaned back on the bench and punched me gently on the arm. "You can be too damn careful."

"Nope."

"Now *there's* a project worth tackling."

What the hell did that mean?

This trip down memory lane was not making any sense. If she wanted something from me, she ought to just ask. I started disassembling the carrier, which had a top half and a bottom half held together by bolts and wing nuts. It was something to do besides avoiding looking at her.

She said, "I'm guessing this will be the first time you've been back since you were a teen. Maybe coming with an adult perspective will change how you see them."

"All of Roger's brothers and sisters and their kids will be looking at me like I'm the skunk at a picnic, only Roger will be lying there dying. What's he going to say to me? 'I'm sorry'? I don't think so. I'm going for Missy and that's it."

"That's a good reason. I'd like to meet her."

Not likely. "Maybe Mandy will talk to me. That would be worth the trip, but I'm not counting on it." I stood up and turned the top of the carrier upside down and nested it into the bottom. It was dark, the park deserted except for us. "I have to get going. I'll walk you to your car."

She stood up and reached toward me, then dropped her hand down. We walked on the path, not touching, not talking, the carrier awkward under my arm. She'd parked the opposite direction from my car. A breeze had finally come up and the air was cool in the darkness. It was late. I should have been on the road an hour ago.

Her car was by a streetlight. I stepped back. "It was good to see you." That was more or less true. And now it was over. Again. Unless she was finally ready to get to the point.

Kate stepped toward me and this time she did put her hand on my arm–electric. "Connie doesn't know everything. I left twice, I think, and you shut me down a week ago. It was bad every time. I can't figure out how to be with you, and I can't walk away and stay gone. It's making me nuts."

"Your family doesn't like me. I've got a weird job. You want someone who's more fun. And who has better housing."

"I was never sure how you felt about me. You never said."

That sat between us, a sad and prickly thing.

Why hadn't I? I took in a breath and tried. "You've seen a bird that's tense and about to fly? That's what you seemed like. One wrong word and you'd be gone. Too risky."

She looked away. "Yeah. Close enough." She drew her shoulders together and then back. "I kind of knew you were really there, but it was hard, being with you. Different. I wanted to hear the words. Connie must be right. I am a fool."

"Well, that makes two of us. We gave it a try."

Her eyes were dark and intense in the vague light. "What if I went with you? To Bellingham? You need someone at your back."

I stared at her. "You'd be, what, my life coach?"

"I was thinking more like your girlfriend." A strand of hair blew across her face.

"Role playing? In a costume?"

"Don't be mean. I'm *asking* to give us another chance. Maybe we can figure this out." She flipped her hair back with a hand. "I can't think of what else to do about you."

I stood motionless in the cool dark while the problems with that blinked to life and winked out. Saying "sure" seemed wrong. No other words came to me.

Kissing her seemed like the best option, so we did that instead, for a long time. The rest could wait.

# About Ann Littlewood

Ann Littlewood was twice the winner of Oregon Writer's Colony first prize for short fiction and has published short stories in *CALYX, A Journal of Art and Literature by Women* and in Scandinavian magazines. She is the author of the Iris Oakley Zoo Mystery series: *Night Kill, Did Not Survive*, and *Endangered,* all from Poisoned Pen Press and available from Amazon. After twelve years as an animal keeper at the Oregon Zoo, she left for a career in corporate America as a business analyst and publications manager. She lives in Portland, Oregon, with her husband and a small but hairy dog. She is active in the Audubon Society of Portland and other tree-hugger organizations.

75963777R00054

Made in the USA
San Bernardino, CA
07 May 2018